STREETZ

Like Sweet Morning Dew

By: Kalibra Edwards

Copyright

***Illustrator**: Craig DynamikFx Smith*

Acknowledgements

First and foremost I must thank God. Without him this would not be possible. I remember when I first started working on this story. I had just lost my job, and I had so much going on. Something told me to write. Well, I started with a special poem, and the rest was history. It took me two years of unemployment and very little support, but I finally finished it. It was hard, but I pushed through because this project was so special to me.

Second I'd like to thank my mother, for bearing with me during these two years. Lord knows how many times she's heard me say, "I'm almost done. I'm so excited!!" She has been my rock all my life and I thank her for believing in me.

Thank you to my sisters, Tina and Jeanette. I love you guys!! They have been my personal cheerleaders. Constantly telling me to finish the book. Are you happy now? Same goes to my family. I love you all and I appreciate you for putting up with me over the years.

Thank you to my fans. I know it's been a while, and I know a lot of you were losing faith that this project would ever be finished, but I'm not a quitter. If I announce it, it will be finished. I don't care what it takes, and for how long. I just really wanted this to be my best work to date. I wanted you guys to feel my heart in the words. I hope you understand.

All My Fellow Authors from Facebook. (Too many to name individually) Thanks for the advice ladies, I wouldn't have gotten through writers block without the tips.

Dedication

Like Sweet Morning Dew…..I took one look at you, and
it was plain to see… You were my Destiny…..

Yo Streetz,

I can hear my heart pumping every time I'm around
you. Your scent drives me insane. How many times will
I allow you to break my heart? There are no words for
shame. I often find myself reminiscing on the days we
used to run a stray. How I miss you. That energy you
kept in my lungs and legs grew wild. Even though it's
been years since I've held you, touched you, in my
dreams sometimes they feel anew. Why didn't I listen
to Granny when she said stay away from boys like you? I
guess like a child discovering the flame on a stove for
the first time, I was just too tempted to touch. From
now until eternity, I'll forever be missing my other half.
Streetz, you're just too much.

<u>Ch.1</u>

Sin

Hook, Line, and Sinker

"All right, everything's processed and in order. Welcome to Gaming Academy Ms. Sinclaire. If you would follow me, I'll give you your tour of the campus." Mr. Robinson said. I tried not to show too much excitement as he led me through the halls of the school. Since I was five years old, I had always had a passion for cards. Learning how to do all kinds of tricks with them was my addiction. It was impossible for you to be a part of my family and not know anything about cards. Every get together, we were either playing dominoes or spades. It was pretty much a ritual.

"This is the Chow hall. You have a lunch card that permits you two hundred a month. Make sure you use it wisely, it has to stretch." I was simply taking everything in. This was so exciting to me. I practically begged my mom to let me go. She didn't want to have to hassle with the loans and payments, but when she saw how excited I was to join, she finally gave in. I was dressed to impress on my first day of school. I had on my yellow form fitting blouse, with faded baby phat jeans. My favorite tan wedged heels were the finishing touch. I was amped.

Once my tour was over and I was pretty much standing around admiring my new atmosphere, I couldn't help but think to myself, This year is gonna be off the hook. I mean, your pretty much playing games all day, How hard can that be? As I browsed through the different tables throughout the room, my excitement went through the roof. There were real casino tables in here. These were tables I was only used to seeing on the casino floors. As I spotted a table being occupied on the second floor, I noticed a dude slinging cards like a professional. When he spotted me, and waved me over, I was intrigued so I followed suit.

He was a skinny, dark chocolate brotha. Skinny jeans wearing swag. Wasn't really my type though, he reminded me more of the geeky weirdo type. The nigga was rocking a book bag for crying out loud. I kept my thoughts to myself. He asked me, "Yo first day?" I nodded yes. I was more of the quiet type. Antisocial, that's the word. I only fucked wit who fucked wit me. "You ever dealt cards before?" he said, "Nah, I've only played lil shit, like go fish and I declare war. I already know what you're thinking. Why would you join a gaming school with no experience in cards?" I laughed to myself. He smiled and said, "They actually like it better that way. It's easier for them to teach you on a clean slate. What's ya name?" I was so busy watching him shuffle the cards, that I didn't hear him. When he asked me again, I looked up and said, "Oh, Sinclaire. What's yours?"

"Tommy, but you can call me T." "How long have you been playing? Shit, you looking like a professional over here." He laughed. That's when I noticed he had some pearly whites. A big smile full of pearly whites. "Believe it or not, I just started like a month ago. I had never played cards before coming here." That threw me for a loop. The game he was dealing was blackjack and how fast he was moving had me hypnotized. "You wanna play?" I looked at him crazy, "Nah, I told you, I don't know how to play any card games." "You've never been to the casinos and played either?" I shook my head no. He passed me some chips and told me where to place the bets. I did. Then he dealt me a hand. I looked at the cards waiting to find out what to do.

"If you want to hit it, tap the table. If you wanna pass, wave over the card." I didn't know what I was hitting, so I hit the table. He threw me down another card. Then I hit again and he took my cards. I was confused. I said, "Why you take my cards?" He laughed and said, "You bust out. I see you have a lot to learn boo," I frowned.

"Well look who we have here?" I turned around and noticed my cousin coming my way. What the hell is she doing here? She sat next to me at the table and I said, "You go here too Kelly? Since when?" She laughed and said, "Girl yeah, I just started last week. You know mama and Shay here too." Just what I needed, a school full of my fam. I already knew we were gonna get into some shit. "Heyyy T," she waved at Tommy. I noticed the change in his attitude from the moment she sat down. I didn't know what that was all about, but once again, I kept my thoughts to myself. "Sup," he said, and continued the game.

"Girl, you know Cortez back in town. We hooked up last night bitch, and that mufucka put in work," I was cracking up. My cousin was one of a kind. She was a light brown, creamy caramel skinned beauty. Her mouth was reckless. She said just what was on her mind and didn't give a fuck who was around to hear it. I noticed Tommy roll his eyes, and I laughed even harder. She got her mouth from her mom though. My cousin Angela was the life of the party at every event. Her and her sister Tangy could turn the fuck up. I was actually glad Angela was going here too, because I knew every day would be a party. Kelly was wearing a tight red shirt, with some blue jean shorts. Her hair was in a curly ponytail with big silver bangle earrings.

"You is a mess girl. I thought you was done wit his ass. Didn't he kick you out on the highway?" She rolled her eyes and said, "Bitch that's old news. He's changed. He said he was just drunk that night. Anyway, he rented a room for the night and was showing off his lil money and shit. Girl you know I had to get me." She got up and started dancing. I was laughing so hard I almost fell off the stool. I heard someone behind us calling Kelly, and just as quick as she came, she was gone. I was still laughing when I noticed Tommy grilling Kelly as she walked off. "Why you looking at her like that?" He went back to the cards and said, "That's yo people?" "Yeah, that's my cousin. Why?" "I can't stand that bitch," My facial expression showed my next question, before I even said it, "Why? What she do to you?" "She just too loud and ghetto," I rolled my eyes. "That's just how she is. What's wrong with being ghetto?"

I mean, he had a lot of nerve talking about people, when his ass walking around looking like the long-lost blue/black ninja turtle. Yeah, I had made it up in my mind, that I was not feeling this asshole. Nobody talked shit about my fam. Family over everything where I'm from. "Well, It was nice meeting you, but I'm bout to slide, it's almost time for classes to start." With that, I left heading to the Chow Hall.

****

After classes were done for the day, I waited outside for my ride. Just thinking about all I had learned in one day was a lot to take in. The games all looked hard and intimidating. I hoped I would be as good as some of my classmates. Looking up from my paperwork I noticed my cousin Kelly and Angela walking towards me. As soon as they reached me, Kelly said, "How you like the school so far? Girl, these games are so easy. Mama been flying through each course." I looked over at Angela to see if it was true, and she was nodding her head also.

"They look so hard. Especially that Roulette. It's so much math, and that was never my strong subject in school." I said, biting my fingernails. It was a bad habit, I had had since I was a child. I did it whenever I was nervous about something. "That shit is as easy as 1-2-3. You know we play games all day long at the house. Whenever you wanna practice, just come through. I'll help you." I planned on taking her up on that offer. I didn't know what to expect. Once I saw my mom's car pulling up, I told them I'd talk to them later.

My mom was dressed and ready for church. I looked at her strangely. "Mom, what are they having at church? We having rehearsal?" I said. She looked in the mirror to check her lipstick and said, "Nope, Mt. Rest is having revival and we have to sing tonight. I'm gonna drop you off at the house. It's food on the stove. Make sure you leave your sister some. I'm eating at the church." She said, warning me. I could eat like it was going out of style. It was ok because it seemed like everything I ate, it never stuck to me. I had a high metabolism. Ever since I was seven, I've had a slim/thick frame. It never changes. I don't have much ass and hips either. I'm getting there though. I always do these butt crunches to try and make it more round. If only I could speed up the process.

"Where's Lala at anyway? You didn't pick her up from school yet?" My little sister was fifteen going on thirty-seven. She swears up and down she's grown. Now once she becomes grown, she'll be wishing she'd enjoyed her childhood. I've always believed a child should stay in a child's place, but that damn Lala though. She was a stunning dark chocolate diva. She got her rich chocolate skin from her dad. I had my mom's color, a rich caramel. "Nah, I haven't went to get her from school yet. I was already on this side of town, so I came to get you first." My mom said as we pulled off.

I started to fill my mom in on all the events that happened today. She was used to my mouth running a mile a minute. She just nodded her head and kept a close eye on the road. As we neared my sisters school I noticed she was wearing my red and black jersey dress.

Oh Hell nah I thought to myself. She wasn't expecting me to be in the car, so when she got in I mugged her hard. She grabbed her head and said, "Ow, Ma, Sin hit me." She whined. I knew she was gonna snitch. "Ma, why she got on my clothes? She always wearing my stuff!!" I was too pissed. Most of the time, my mom would just let us argue back and forth. It was always Latavia's word against mine.

"Lala, Why are you wearing your sisters clothes? This isn't the first time you've snuck out the house with her clothes." I noticed her rolling her eyes and I wanted to smack them out the socket. "I was in a rush, and I thought this one was mine." She snickered which made me even more angry. "You went in my room, in my drawer, but you thought it was yours. Girl," I wanted to slap her so bad. I had to pray to keep my temper down. My little sister could always irk that last nerve of mine. When we pulled into the driveway, she rushed out of the car and into the house. I don't know why she thought she'd get off that easily, because I was far from done with her. As mom pulled off to head to church, I smiled inwardly. Yea, I'm a sneaky lil bitch.

I went directly into her room and grabbed the first cute outfit I saw out of her drawer. "Oo, I think this will be cute for tomorrow." I said walking out of her room. I was giggling to myself when my sister tackled me from behind. We landed on the floor with a hard thud. "Give it back!!! That's my new Ivy Park Outfit!!" I was grabbing for the first thing I saw. I noticed a stuffed bear next to me on the floor. I grabbed it and popped her in the eye from behind. I must have put some muscle into it because she was holding her eye screaming, "Owwww, My eye." I didn't give a durn. I got up grabbing my neck. That little twit had a good grip. "If you wanna be petty all ya life, I can be petty too. Stay the fuck out my shit, and I'll leave your shit alone." With that I headed into the kitchen to fix our plates for dinner.

<u>**Ch.2**</u>

Streetz

It's Hard Out Here for A Pimp

"Shit, I can't ride wit that much work down there nigga," Every time I deal wit this mufucka, It's always something. "My nigga, that ain't but five ounces. You know them fuckas ain't gon stop you for no green." Donte was trying to get off some ganga. Problem was, we were in Jackson, and he wanted me to drive it down to Gulfport. I'm five months out the joint. I wasn't gonna press my luck trying that bull. Not to mention, I still don't have a lick of license. "You try that dummy mission if you want to nigga. You know I'm fresh out. I ain't going back for nobody. Just give me my regular and I'm straight." He could tell I wasn't budging, so he started to break down my original stash.

"What yawl got in this mufucka to eat? Shit, I'm hungry den a mugg." I rubbed my belly walking in the kitchen in search of snacks. "Damn, Toya ass ain't cook tonight?" I said, once I saw there was no meals in the microwave. "Shit, you know Toya in one of her fawnky ass moods whenever food ain't on the stove. Caught a bitch textin me, talkin bout suckin me up. You know her ass went through the roof. I had some heavy making up to do." This nigga was laughing at the shit. I don't play that. I would've smacked the fuck out a bitch. "Yo, I know you handled that bitch." He laughed and said, "Hell nah.

Shit, Shawty got the jaws of life my nigga," This fool. I couldn't help laughing at his dumbass. "I already know she breaking you off then. How much bread she working wit? Cuz I ain't fuckin up home unless a bitch got that dough."

I propped my feet up on his living room table. "She go to school at JSU to be a nurse. You know she got that bread young," We both laughed. As he rolled a blunt, he said, "And guess what my nigga? She got a twin too. The bitch bad, so you already know her sis bad." Now that caught my attention. I wasn't expecting that. "Oh word? She stay out here?" He nodded passing me the joint. "Hell yeah, and she just broke up wit her dude last week. I met her a couple times. She cool. They Puerto Rican." I didn't know how I felt about her being Puerto rican, most of those bitches are crazy. "Set something up my nigga, I'll see whats up." I puffed and passed him the joint. I had to get out of there and go get something to eat. This nigga was trippin. "I'm bout to head to Mickey D's. You want a burger or something?" He was zooted. He looked at me laughing and said, "Hell nah nigga, I got my own bread if I want a burger mufucka," he passed me a twenty and gave me his order.

As I stepped outside walking to my car, I started to think on where my life was headed. I don't know why I kept taking these chances. I knew how dangerous this game was. At any moment I could be taken from my family. Shit, when bills gotta be paid, and babies have to be fed, a mufucka gotta do what he gotta do. It wasn't like I would be hired anywhere with felon on my app. Baby moms in my ear every month about the rent. Nah, I had to make some shit shake. I called James to see if he had any gigs lined up.

"Aye James, anything in the lineup? I'm down bad right now. I'm trying to make some shit shake, ya feel me?" I said. I heard loud voices in the background so I figured he was still at the school. "Yeah, but it's in Mobile. I don't know if you wanna take that long of a drive. It's a week-long gig." I laughed because he knew where my mind was before I even said it. "Hell nah, that's too far. I see you getting it in on the weekend. What yall having a tournament?" I said fishing for more info. "Nah, it's just practice for the upcoming tournament. Randy said he's looking at you to deal for next season. You think you can handle it?" This was the break I needed. "You already know I'm down bruh. Just tell me when and where. I'm there." I heard him talking to someone in the background, then he said to me, "Alright, I'll hit you up when we start practice for next season. They need me back at the table now. They act like they can't do a thing without me over their shoulder." I laughed and said goodbye before hanging up.

Riding through downtown Jackson brought hella memories back to mind. This was my stomping grounds. I was born and raised here, but a nigga had to relocate cuz it was getting too hot. I figured Gulfport would be a good spot to start over. My girl was already down there. So I just said fuck it, I'll join the card school to try and get a good job. I didn't think I would like it as much as I did. I caught on quickly when they taught me how to deal. I knew it would only be a matter of time before I got my first dealing job. James, my instructor, who was also my homey, had put me on to a couple under the table card gigs. He knew my history with the law. After I stopped at McDonalds and was heading back to Donte's, he called telling me he talked to the girls. They wanted us to meet them at Club Level tonight. I wasn't too fond of the club scene. That's how too many niggas got caught up. It was an easy place to become a target. You could easily get sidetracked. Never the less, I told him I was down.

****

*If you know me……Know this ain't my fungshway…..
Certified Everywhere …. Ain't gotta print my resume ……
Talking crazy….. I pull up Andale…… R.I.P to Nate
Dogg…… I had to regulate -Migos*

Walking into Club Level, I noticed all the different variations of people in the room. Most were the usual club boppers who were there from sundown to sunup. The stunners, who were in V.I.P trying to show up everyone in attendance. The pill poppers, sweating in the middle of the dance floor. I was already ready to go. I had seen enough. "Where ya girl at bruh?" He pulled his phone out and looked at a few messages. "She say they coming through the doors now. Chill out mayne. You need a drink?" "You damn right, I'll be right back." I went over to the bar and got two shots of hen. When I made it back to Donte, he was standing next to a light skinned Chris brown looking mufucka. "Waddup," he said. I wasn't quick to add niggas to my circle, so I looked at Donte for an explanation. "This my nigga Ron, we grew up together. He told me, he moving to Gulfport next month, and was trying to get on." I looked him up and down.

"Waddup, You old enough to even be in here nigga?" Ron looked around, proving my point that he was underage. "I'm good. I'm in here, ain't I?" He had spunk. I liked that. I guess I'll let him make it. He was rocking some timbs with a blue and black coogi fitted. "How long he been down? Is he thorough? Cuz you already know I ain't wasting my time with anything that doesn't have potential." Donte vouched without blinking an eye. "I wouldn't come to you with nothing less my nigga," I trusted Donte with my life, so I knew if he vouched then ole boy was trust worthy. I dapped him up and we made plans to link up when he touched down.

By the time the girls had made it over to us, I was four shots in, and feeling good. I can't even front, Shawty was bad. She looked to be about five feet seven inches in heels. My eyes had zeroed in on all that ass in that sexy two-piece outfit she was rocking. She sashayed over to me, and said, "Hi, you must be Streetz. I'm Helena. Donte's description didn't do you justice." Shit, I didn't wanna toot my own horn, but I thought I was looking pretty dapper in my fresh white jordans, clean white tee, and coogi jeans. I leaned into her ear and said, "You wanna dance boo?" When she smiled showing off her dimples, I started to walk her toward the dance floor.

As August Alsina's Porn star played through the speakers, shawty put in work. I swayed with her every move to try and keep up with her. When she winded her hips and turned around looking at me over her shoulder, I was ready to dick her down on the dance floor. That hen in my system was fuckin wit me. I knew she liked what she was feeling cuz she bent over and gyrated on me harder. When she came back up, I whispered in her ear, "Let me holla at you real quick," I walked her over to the bathroom area, and she pulled me in the girls room. She wasted no time pulling my man out and gobbling it like it was her last supper. She got real nasty wit it. Gotdamn lil mama

When she came up for air, I brushed her hair out of her face and she went back in. She even gobbled my balls up. When I couldn't take anymore and felt myself having a heart attack in the bathroom of the club, I picked her up and put her on the sink. "Damn," I said, pulling a condom out my back pocket. She was smiling and wiping her mouth. "I take it you like that Papi," That papi shit got me every time. With the jimmy in place, I had her up against the sink. "Ay Papi, yes," I gripped her hair with my left while holding her in place with my right. I guess she liked that rough shit cuz she said, "Ooo shit, fuck me harder Papi, yesss, like that," I gave her a few more strokes and put her down, then she turned around. I was just about to enter her from behind when a girl walked in. "Well Damn," she said.

Lena got out of character, and cussed ol girl out. "Get the fuck out bitch," I knew she was going to be a problem. The way she was being possessive. That didn't stop me from catching that nut though. We picked up where we left off but I pushed her into one of the stalls just in case someone else came in. When I felt it building, I pulled out and finished in the toilet. I didn't take any chances fuckin wit bitches. I went back in search of Donte and the crew. Helena was right behind me walking on wobbly legs.

<u>Ch. 3</u>

Sin

A Wolf in Sheep's Clothing

I had just started my first week of Roulette. I was failing miserably. I hated this game with a passion. I just couldn't get it. I passed Blackjack with no problem. I think it's because of all the extra calculations with this game. I never was the best in math class. My cousin Kelly and James, my instructor, was trying to coach me on different ways I can approach each problem.

"Look at it this way, whenever you see reds, you know they'll be even. When you see blacks, you know they'll be odd. Don't let the stacks scare you. All you have to do is break them down. Then solve them." James was so cool and laid back. He always took his time with teaching us the games. For some reason, it felt like my brain just got stuck whenever I saw those high ass stacks. Even now watching him break the stacks down, my brain was still on stuck. Kelly was rolling the dice for the game, while I tried to deal it.

Once the bell rang signaling class was over, I was so happy to get outside for break. I needed some fresh air. When I passed the craps table, I noticed the weird kid eyeing me again. I ignored him walking outside to the patio. He followed me and stopped me before I sat down. "Can I holla at ya real quick?" he said. I wanted to say no, but my curiosity got the best of me. I followed him to the side of the building. I wondered why he needed to be so secluded.

"Wassup?" I said. He looked around and leaned into me saying, "You know anyone taking Percs?" I frowned and said, "No," I started to walk off, and he asked me, "Can you call around and ask for me?" I said no, and the puppy dog eyes he gave me, made me give in. I called a few friends and family, and everyone said no. Then my aunt Rose said yes, which shocked the hell out of me, because she had always talked smack about me dilly dallying with drugs of any kind. He told me to pass him the phone, and I listened in on the convo while they talked.

"I got dat for the six, whats good?" he said, I couldn't hear her response, but he said, "Word? I'll be through there in a minute. I'll bring Sin," then he looked at me and said, "Is that cool wit you? You'll roll wit me to your aunts?" I nodded yes, anything to get away from class. He wrapped up the convo and we made our way to his ride. As we rode in silence, I had to admit, I liked his calm, and cool demeanor. Out of nowhere he asked me, "How you get back and forth to school Sin?" I said, "My aunt usually drops me off and my mom picks me up. Since they both work, sometimes I miss days." He nodded his head and said, "If you want, I can come scoop you in the mornings and drop you off. I don't stay too far from you."

I was happy to hear that, because that would take the strain off my mother. When we pulled up to my aunts, she came to the door. He told me to stay in the car, because it would only take a second. I was glad, because I didn't want to be involved in whatever they had going on. While I was sitting in the car, my nosiness got the best of me. I noticed he had a car seat in the backseat. So, he has a family. He looked like the type to always have someone. He wasn't that bad looking, I guess I just never paid much attention because of his nasty attitude. When he came back to the car, I asked him, "How many kids do you have?" "I just had my first. She'll be four months tomorrow." He stared ahead. I smiled and said, "That's great, kids are a blessing. You should be proud." He laughed and said, "I am, trust me. I am. She's everything to me."

We stopped at a couple places before reaching my house. For some reason, I wasn't ready to leave. Our ride was so smooth and just comfy, I found myself asking him, "Where you going when you drop me off?" He turned the radio down and said, "I gotta make a few runs in Bay Saint Louis," I was intrigued and again found myself asking, "Can I ride with you?" He looked around and said, "I don't think that would be a good idea. You can't handle the shit I'm into. I won't put you in harm's way." I was disappointed, and wanted to fuss with him, but the look he gave me told me to chill. I was angered with myself for even asking him those questions. It was something pulling me toward him and I didn't like it at all.

****

A few hours after school, my mom and sister still hadn't made it home, so I decided to go for a walk. I figured now would be as good a time as any to go visit my cousin so she could help me with a few roulette problems. That game literally was exhausting. When I made it to rich avenue, there were cars all down the street. I was wondering what was going on. I knew there was always a party going on at Kelly's house, but It was never this deep. Maybe someone else is throwing a party I thought to myself. Kelly came outside dressed in a baby pink haulter and low cut booty short blue jeans. Kelly was always dressed to impress. I looked down at my orange Juicy couture mid riff short sleeved shirt, with my khaki mini skirt and knew it must run in our genes. We were undeniably fly.

When she reached me, I asked her, "What's with all the cars Keke?" She was checking someone out across the street. "Girl, Roxanne bald headed ass decided she was gonna throw a party after she found out about mine. I told that bitch she didn't wanna try it with me. I'd set that bitch on fire if I wasn't still on probation." I laughed, because my crazy ass cousin would definitely do it. She had a rap sheet a mile long. She only got caught on a bullshit shoplifting charge. If they really knew the things my cuz got into, she would be on Rikers Island somewhere.

Growing up in the projects, Kelly didn't have it easy. She was what you called, a victim of her environment. I figured the reason we were so close is because we had so much in common. The things we went through were similar in every way. From being raped at a young age, to becoming women before our time. We were forced into a world of prostitution by circumstance. I had been kicked out of the house since I was fourteen. Eventually I was reaching out for love, and the streets accepted me with open arms. Whenever my mom would allow me back home, she never knew the mental scars embedded within me.

"If you don't get your hot-headed ass in the house. That's why you in trouble now. Making bad decisions. I bet you'll think twice about hitting Walmart from now on." I laughed. She rolled her eyes and said, "Bitch, I just need a better game plan. My guard was down that time." We laughed as we walked into the smoke-filled house. It seemed as though everyone had decided to come out today. Observing my surroundings, I noticed my cousins all sitting around the table playing spades. That was always the game of choice and yet, I still can't play. Anytime I ask to join in, they ignore my request. I felt so violated.

"Bam, Deuce is spade. Give me my pair. We got this Sis," Angela yelled across the table to her twin sister Tangy. When she jumped up to high five her, I knew I would be in for a long night. Whenever they got to playing spades, they could be at it for hours. I followed Kelly into the kitchen. My cousins Shay and Bebe were sitting at the table eating hotdogs. Kelly went to fix us a hotdog and noticed there weren't any more wieners. "B, I told you to save me one. Damn, who ate my stuff?"

Bebe looked around innocently. "Girl ain't nobody touched your food. It's in the microwave dummy." Kelly rolled her eyes and walked back to the microwave to fix our food.

"So I hear you crushin on Tommy. Why you like that fool?" Shay said looking up at me from her plate. I laughed so hard. "I never said I liked his ass. Who told you that? Kelly?" I looked back at Kelly grilling the back of her head. "I didn't say anything. I just said ya'll were cute. Shay you talk too damn much." They were laughing and I didn't find it funny anymore. "That nigga is too arrogant for my taste. What he got against you Kelly? He was grilling you when you walked off the other day." Kelly hunched her shoulder and handed me my plate. "He never said anything to me about it. I thought he was cool." I looked back and forth between her and Shay. I could tell it was something they weren't telling me, but I decided to let it go for now. "Whatever though, but what's his story anyway? He's such a weirdo, and why is his ass always wearing that damn book bag?" We bust out laughing. Everyone noticed the chocolate kid in the book bag at school. "Hell yeah, every time I see him he got on that lime green ass book bag. Looking like a middle schooler on his way to class." Kelly said. We were dying laughing. We didn't even notice Tangy come in the kitchen.

"Where the hell yall bitches going? Going to sell that twat?" She was sipping on some Taaka Vodka. I eased next to her and rubbed her shoulder a little and said, "What you sippin on cuz. You already know what time it is," I laughed and she snatched her arm away. "Girl, if you don't get yo young ass away from me. You not about to have your mama beating down my door. Hell nah," I gave her the sweetest puppy eyes I could muster. "I'm grown Cuz, I'm eighteen and a half." She laughed in my face. How disrespectful. "Girl, you have two years until your grown. Don't be so quick to jump now." I rolled my eyes and tried to walk away. She grabbed my arm pulling me back, offering me a few hits. It burned down my throat. I knew the effect it would have on me later, so I wasn't tripping. I could hear Kelly yapping about Roxanne again. I had a feeling something was about to go down.

"Nah, I say we go over there and pop off. You know how we do Sis." Bebe said to Kelly. Kelly was the oldest of four. There was Kelly, her brother Yayo, and her little sisters Bebe, and Coco. Yayo was the only male so he often took on the role of the oldest. At the moment, they were all sitting in the kitchen, plotting on how they would handle Roxanne. Roxanne was a tall, busty, high yella stallion. She was inDd too grown for her own good. Every time I saw Roxanne in high school she was half naked. The school admin had placed her on suspension many times for being inappropriately dressed. She was who you would call a free spirit. I'm sure if it was allowed she would go everywhere in her birthday suit. Everyone often wondered why she acted the way she did. Her parents were two of the richest blacks in the city. Her mom was a lawyer and her dad a county judge. I couldn't for the life of me, figure out why she chose to get an apartment in the hood. I don't know, maybe she liked that thug life.

I was trying to keep my heart steady, because I just knew I was about to get into something. Every time my cousins rolled up on someone together, it usually didn't end well. When I saw the crowd of people gathered in her apartment, I understood why she liked the ghetto so much. There were couples seated everywhere in the living room. Most of them fondling each other. I could hear Yo Gotti pumping through the speakers. Everyone had a cup in their hands. It was lit, I had to give it to her, she could throw a party.

"Yo where Roxy at?" Kelly said, taking charge. The couple pointed to the back. They didn't really pay too much attention to us, as they were tonguing each other down. We walked through the halls stopping at each door. Most rooms were filled with blunts or unspeakable acts. We finally found Roxanne in the last door. She looked surprised to see us. Yeah, she knew what time it was whenever Kelly comes with her entourage. She was posted on the bed with two guys and a girl. They had been passing a doobie and drinking. She frowned and said, "Wassup Kelly, why yall rolling up on me like this? The parties in the front room."

Kelly didn't do too much talking, which was why I was surprised she answered Roxanne. She looked back at us and then to Roxy. "You trying me bitch. Now I know you knew my fucking party was tonight. Every time I turn around yo ass is jocking my style. I've seen you in at least five of my wardrobe choices. I never said anything because I figured you needed a role model." Everyone laughed. Roxy turned red from embarrassment. She got up to get in Kelly's face and Bebe slapped her down before Kelly could buck. As her friend got up from the bed to help her, I grabbed her by the hair and said, "I don't think you wanna do that." Kelly knelt next to a scared Roxanne and whispered, " I told you not to fuck wit me." As she stood up, she delivered a swift kick to Roxy's gut. Yayo mean mugged the boys sitting on the bed. They knew Yayo's rap sheet so they didn't try anything. As we filed out of the room, we could hear Roxy yelling, "I'mma see you bitch, I put that on everything I love!"

<u>Ch.4</u>

Streetz

Baby Mama Drama

"What they say at the doctor?" I had dropped Belle off at the doctor this morning, since it was right next to her job, she walked the distance to work. She was in the kitchen finishing up dinner. She rolled her eyes at my question. I already knew shit was about to hit the fan. She didn't even look at me when she said, "I'm five months pregnant T. I didn't know, because I thought we were careful after I had Lashia. Shit makes sense though, all the sickness lately." *Oh, Shit* I knew I couldn't have heard right, so I said, "What'd you say?" She continued plating the food and said, "You heard me, I'm pregnant and it's a boy. There's no reason to trip about it now. I told you before, that it was too early to do anything, but like always, you didn't listen. Now look where we are." She turned and faced me. I was too shocked to speak.

"What the fuck T? Two kids? We can barely take care of the one we have. I don't know if I can do this shit. Especially with your ass always on the go. You're never hear when I need you. You get on my nerves." She yelled. I went to grab her around her waist. She kept pushing me away, and I told her, "You can't be stressing boo. Especially not right now. We're gonna get through this together. You know I'm gonna do what I have to, to take care of home. Just trust me ok." She went back to plating the food. "Where have you been? I know school didn't last until seven tonight." I couldn't tell her I had gotten caught up with the time. I was enjoying the vibe with shorty earlier and wasn't ready for her to leave. I made random stops just for alone time with her. I don't know what it was about her, but she was just different.

"JT came up on a lick earlier. He's setting the shit up now, and later he'll be back by so we can ride out and handle that." I breathed a sigh of relief when she didn't reply. I didn't need any more problems than the ones we were already facing. JT was my vanilla homey from the school. He hooked me up from time to time with some work. He helped me get in good with the folks at the casinos. We hit them for a lick almost every month. I was so good, there were supervisors telling me I had a guaranteed job there when I finish school. I was the life of the party. I'm a Casanova by right.

"You know I don't like him. You stay in trouble rolling wit that fool." She said. She's referring to the one time we got caught. That incident really had nothing to do with JT, it was my ganja we got caught with. She blames him because I was riding with him at the time. I swear she acts like my mother. I don't know if it's the Cancer sign in her, or if it's just her. "If you remember correctly, I was the one who was caught slipping that night. JT was probably the reason I walked away scott free. Them mufuckas would've threw my black ass under the jail, feel me?" She was still pissed, so I got no response. As soon as I started to get in her ass about ignoring me, Lashia started crying from the living room. She was playing with her toys in the playpen while Belle finished cooking. I went to get up and Belle looked at me as if I had three heads. "I got her, why don't you sit here and figure out how we gon take care of another mouth to feed." She said nastily. Damn, I had really fucked up. I knew it was gonna take some heavy making up on my part tonight. I thought quickly on how I was gonna handle this situation. Nine times out of ten, if I tried to get it, she won't be wit it. I smiled thinking of how I was gonna change her mind.

"Aww, it's ok. Mommy's here. That baby was scared? Aww, mom and dad were just talking that's all." She said. She looked over at me as I entered the living room and said, "You scared her with all that yelling you were doing. I told you we should work on not arguing in front of her. I don't want her becoming stressed out because of drama in the home." As she rubbed Kalashia's back whispering baby coos, she was grilling me the entire time. The stare was so icy, I felt the cold chill in my bones. I wiped my hands down my face in frustration. "Say bay, lets get Lashia to bed early tonight. Then we can pick up this conversation. I had a long day, and I know you're stressed from work and tending to Laylay." She rolled her eyes and walked into the kitchen placing Kalashia in her high chair.

With our plates on the table, we finished our food in silence. I didn't know what was going through her mind, but I could only imagine. She never once held eye contact with me, which meant she was beyond pissed. I don't know why I didn't pull out that night. She was right, she did tell me it was too early. I had a high sex

34

drive so, once I was in, there was no stopping me. To keep the tension from eating at me, I turned my attention to my daughter. She was my stress reliever throughout each day. Whenever I had a bad day, her smile could light up my world. Her giggles were medicine to my soul. As I fed her meal to her, she giggled in between bites. "Come on girl, stop playing and eat your food." I laughed while feeding her peas and rice.

Once Lay Lay was put to bed and I was out of the shower, Belle decided to soak in a hot bath. She had been in there for a good hour before I went to check on her. "You alright in here?" I said peeking my head in the door. She had fallen asleep in the tub. I knew her weariness was from all she did in a day. I admired her strength. When I lost my job last year and was in and out of jail, she was always there holding me down. I know she talked a lot of shit sometimes, but she had a nigga's back no matter what.

I washed her up and dried her body, before placing her snuggly in bed for the night. I guess my plan for tonight would have to wait. When I figured, she was in a deep sleep, I slipped out of the room, to make a call to my boy JT. "Yo my man, where ya at?" I said walking into the kitchen. "I'm in B-town right now whoa. You ready for me to scoop ya?" He said, letting me know everything was good with the pickup. "Yeah, I'll be ready. Don't forget to stop at Quan's and get that other flava. He called me an hour ago." He knew I meant the other package from Quan. "Damn, I forgot all about Quan, bruh. I'll stop through there, I should charge that fool gas money." He laughed. As long as he wasn't looking for shit from me, I was cool.

An hour later we were on our way to Big D's house. He was a new cat around the way. He's just starting out in the hood, so he's trying to make a name for himself. He had asked me if I could hook him up with some fire and a few burners. I told him the shit wouldn't be cheap, but I would work with him. I made sure I carried my dessert eagle on me. They didn't call this nigga Big D for nothing. He looked to be as big as Heavy D and the gang. I worked out from time to time, but I was still a small guy. I knew going toe to toe with him would be a waste of my time. JT, he may stand a chance, but not ya boy.

"What it do, Streetz?" D said when he opened the door. "Not shit my nigga. Tryna make this paper. Ya feel me?" He embraced me and gave JT a once over before looking at me. "Oh, this my boy JT. He cool, you good yo." He looked at him suspiciously and led us into the house. I was surprised at how neat he kept his trap house. Everything was organized and put in place. He had workers in the kitchen cooking up goodies, while his girls were on the living room couches, packaging. We followed him into the back room to talk business.

"So, you know the score, You got that for me?" I said, not one to beat around the bush. "My man Larry got you covered. How much we talkin?" I frowned and said, "I got an ounce, was that not the deal?" He laughed it off, and I could feel the energy in the room change. I looked over at JT because I knew something didn't feel right. D noticed the exchange and said, "Relax bruh, You already know I don't get down like that. Larry give em they shit." A tall lanky fella walked over with a stack of bands in his hand. When I noticed his hand behind his back, I drew first, "Yo my man, why you trying me? Try to help a lil nigga out, and this is the thanks I get? Yea, I knew yall New yitty mufuckas would be on some fuck shit. JT get that shit yo," JT snatched the money from Larry's hands while I kept my gun trained on D.

"I'm disappointed in you my man, I thought we were gonna be good business partners." I shook my head while heading out the door. By the time we made it to the car, Big D and his flunky were firing shots. JT was pulling off as I let shots out from the window. "Damn bruh. How many times am I gonna get into some shit with your ass man." JT laughed as we drove away. I laughed looking out the window paranoid. That was close. I told JT to rush me to the house, cuz I knew the block was about to get hot.

<u>Ch 5</u>

Sin

Thug Holiday

I was finishing up my test to move on from Roulette. I knew I had aced it. I finally figured a smooth technique to get me through the game. Now I was a pro. I could count the stacks as if there was only one chip on the board. James was proud of me. He constantly told me how he believed in me. I knew I had to stay on the ball. "It's like riding a bicycle. Once you get it, it's stuck with you for life. You've got this. The more you continue to practice, the better you'll be. If you could stay focused and keep your head out of those fairy tale books you carry around, you'd be alright." He said pointing at my newest novel sitting on the table next to me.

"I hear you Mr. James, but I love reading. That would be really hard to do." I said smiling back at him. James was an older, middle aged man. His personality was a lot younger than his actual age. We often joked, calling him player of the year because he was always around women. Young, Black, White, Puerto Rican, or Haitian, he loved them all. "Well if you don't give them a break, there's no way you'll make it through craps in two weeks. That game has to have your full attention or you'll be lost." He said with determination in his eyes. I didn't want to let him down. I nodded and said, "I got

38

you Mr. J" I laughed and headed in the direction of the Chow hall.

I noticed Shay sitting in the back of the hall eating by herself, so I join her. I know I call Shay my cousin, but she's only my play cousin. My auntie is best friends with her mom. Since we were kids, we just became accustomed to calling her our cousin. She looked up at me when I sat down and said, "Wassup Chick. You must've got out of class early. How'd you do on your test? I think I failed mine. I can't even lie, that bitch was hard." I laughed and said, "Girl, I aced that lil shit. What I'm worried about is craps coming up in two weeks. I don't think I'm ready." She shook her head while stuffing a forkful of mashed potatoes in her mouth. She was eating like a slob. You would think she hadn't eaten in a month. "Slow down girl, it's not going anywhere," I laughed and she punched me playfully in the arm. " Shutup B, you want some? You looking pretty heavy at my food. Why you ain't just go get you a plate?" I smirked and said, "If I wanted a plate, I would be eating right now. I was only trying to get out of class while I wait for Tommy to get back." I noticed her rolling her eyes, and I quickly added, "What was that for?" she didn't look up when she said, "I didn't say anything. Just thinking that's all. How well do you know Tommy anyway?"

"I don't know him too well, but shit, he's been nice enough to help me out, and that's all that matters. Why you ask that though?" I said cocking my head to the side. She continued to eat her food as if I hadn't said a word. "Go ahead and tell me, since you brought it up.

What's good on him?" She finally looked up from her plate and said, "You know I'm cool with his baby mama. Her name is Belle. We used to be best friends, I knew her because we went to the same high school. I was there when she first met Tommy. She was staying with her aunt in Bradbury apartments over on Canal. I was staying with them. We had met Tommy and this dude named Donte one day at the mall. Once they started dating, Donte and I started messing around. Whenever I snuck Donte over, he brought Tommy too. Her aunt didn't play," She laughed. I was so intrigued, I just told her to keep going.

"We were all so close. We were chilling hard, like every day. One day, I accidently slept with Tommy. Belle didn't know, so we just acted like it never happened. When we went to the pool one day, Belle had found out about it. How? I don't even know, but we got to fighting. Tommy broke the fight up and I packed my stuff and left that night. That dude is bad news. He's always in trouble. He was in and out of jail the whole time I knew him. Belle kept taking him back though. I'm just telling you this, to tell you to watch your back with that fool. He will try you." I couldn't help but laugh.

"Girl, there is nothing like that going on. We're just friends. He been helping me out from time to time. No biggie." She shook her head. I guess she didn't believe me, but oh well. It's the truth. Yeah, he was cute and all, but he had too much drama going on in his life. I thought to myself How do you accidently sleep with somebody? I laughed. I told her I was about to head out to the break area. She said, she'd be out when she finished her food.

Kelly and her friend Myra were seated on the table outside when I walked up. I said, "Ya'll out early too?" They nodded. They were looking through their phones. When Kelly started playing Jshin and Latocha Scotts "One Night Stand", I went to singing along with them. We all burst out singing at the chorus. *You say you're having my baby, but I don't know if it's mine. It all started from a one-night stand, it wasn't part of the plan. Now I see you got an attitude, and your so confused. You didn't tell me about your man at home, so what ya gonna do*

I hadn't noticed Tommy walk up after the song ended. We were all so hyped. Myra played her song next: *Early one morning, while you were asleep. I received a letter, but there was no addressee. So I paid it no mind in fact, I wanted to send it back, but something that I was feeling said open it. It said dear reader, once close friend of mine, I hope that this letter, finds you in time. Cuz your love is ending and my life's just beginning, with a woman that I know you hold dear to you, and it made me wanna say.........*

We were all joking about Kelly getting a letter, and she said, "Bitch please, I would have been in jail if my homegirl sent me a letter like that. She would've been six feet under and I would've castrated ole boy. I don't play that shit." We all laughed. Since Tommy was the only guy outside, he made a face and grabbed his jewels. "Thanks for mentioning it. Just fuck my mental up, why don't ya." He said. I played my song next.

I was so into it, I sang along. *Just like the soldiers that ain't coming home this year, just like the fellas in prison. We miss you so much for real. What about the children, who ran away, that ain't coming home today. Here's a message from coast to coast. When them thugs really need it the most, A thug Holiday* I was shocked to hear Tommy come in on Tricks part: *Just like, Just like* I smiled extra wide. I loved to sing, and for him to join in, made it even more special. I may have been feeling him just a little. Then he asked me if my aunt had called and I was right back to being annoyed with his ass. Almost every day it never failed, he asks me if my aunt called about his product. Most of the time I would just call her in front of him, and let him talk business. He could bug the hell out of a person. It was so annoying, but I knew it was just a part of the line of work he was in.

I turned and noticed Shay coming to join us outside. I was sitting next to Tommy on the bench. Shay looked at Tommy and said, "Wassup Streetz," I looked at Tommy confused. I was about to say who's streets when he nodded and said, "Waddup," I looked at him and softly asked, "Who's Streetz? Is that another nickname of yours?" he looked off smoking on his cigarette and replied, "That's nobody. It's somebody I used to be. I'm changing my life for the better. I told you, that was why I made the move down here to begin with." I knew when he didn't want to push things so I let it go. I decided to ask him about something else that was on my mind instead, "So you and Shay cool?" he looked at me trying to figure out where I was going with this, and said, "Nah, I know her, but we ain't cool." I bit my lip and thought hard about my next question. I don't know why it even bothered me to know. I just said, What the hell, whats the worst thing he could say? "T, have you and Shay ever messed around?" There, I had gotten it out. He didn't blink an eye when he said, "Leave that alone. That's in the past."

That was my answer. I knew from his answer that it was true what Shay said. Now, in my mind, I'm thinking, I wonder what really went down in that whole situation. I know Tommy will never tell me. Why did I give a fuck anyway? For some reason, Tommy had begun to become a beautiful mystery to me, and I just wanted to piece all his pieces of the puzzle together. Again, don't ask me why, because I swear I can't stand this peanut headed nigga.

****

Tommy was supposed to drop me off at home, but when he noticed my aunts' car in the drive way he got out also. This was the first time he had ever been inside my house. I was a little nervous of what he thought about my living space. Our home was a modest three bedrooms, two bath house. We had come a long way from the projects we had once lived in. Judging from the way he stared at all our nice furnishings, I took it he liked the place. My aunt was in the kitchen talking on her cell phone when he walked in.

"Oh Johnny, let me call you back.... No, It's not another nigga ...... You know I only have eyes for you boo" I noticed my aunt snickering with her hand over the phone. I laughed at her silly self. People wonder where I get it from. I came from the most beautifully orchestrated family ever created. Yes, we all have big egos. Our confidence can sometimes be out of this world. Blame it on my grandmother. She was a woman who believed in catering to your man, but also, independence if he chose to leave.

"What ya got fa me youngin," my aunt said to Tommy. He motioned for her to step outside on the porch. I guess he didn't like talking business in front of me. I don't know why though, because I did half the runs with him every morning before he dropped me off at school. As they were leaving, my sister was coming in the door. Latavia looked him up and down, then frowned. I knew she had instantly dubbed him a bum. Being that she was raised with sort of a silver spoon in her mouth, my sister didn't understand the hood life. Tommy was every bit of a thrown away, hoodlum living child. He was living life on the edge, not because he had a choice. It was the cards he was dealt. From the average eye, though, he was a sexy, charming, gentleman. Not many got to see the savage beast behind the smile. I'll never forget the day I got a glimpse.

He had just picked me up from class. His friend Marcus was seated in the passenger seat. I sat silent, while I listened in on their conversation. "Yo, that punkass nigga gon get his bruh. I don't see how you let that bitch go." Tommy was quiet as he concentrated on the road. Marcus continued to ramble. "How you let him make it wit that disrespect bruh?" Tommy's head damn near swerved off his shoulders in response.

"I ain't let him make it with shit. I got it handled. I got something for that ass, trust." I could feel the tension fill the car. When I noticed one of my favorite songs on the radio, I reached to turn it up. Tommy and I had the same tastes in music, which was why I always picked the station we listened to when we rode. Once I sat back and started nodding to the beat, Tommy had turned the radio off. "Why you do that? That was my jam," I whined. "Don't touch my shit." I snapped my head and said, "What? You never had a fucking problem with me touching your shit before. Now you wanna front cuz ya dude in the car." He stared in my eyes through the rearview mirror. I knew there had to have been flames burning in mine.

"You know you could always walk." He said still staring me down. I was beyond pissed. I grabbed for the handle and told him to stop the car. He hurried and locked the doors before saying, "Man sit yo crazy ass back bruh. Why the fuck you always playing for?" He laughed. I was still heated so I mean mugged him the whole ride home.

That was the first time I had saw that angry side of him. I didn't like it at all. It gave me pause. Made me reconsider my dealings with him. When he had finished conducting his business with my Aunt Rose, he came back in the kitchen and whispered, "Aye, who was that girl?" I cocked a brow and finished up my sandwich saying, "None of ya business. That's who," He laughed and said, "Come on bruh, quit blocking." This was what I hated about being friends with him. My emotions were all over the place. One minute, I couldn't stand him, and the next minute, I was red with envy at the women in his life. I never said anything because I didn't want to ruin our friendship. He had another thing coming if he thought he was going to try to holla at my sister.

"Boy bye! You might as well dead that lil shit." He was thirty-eight hot with me. I didn't give a fuck though. Who did he think I was? First of all, I'm not hooking my little sister up with anyone, period. Second of all, with his pedigree and everything I've learned about him so far, he didn't have a chance in hell. I laughed and walked into the living room. When I heard the front door close, I knew he was gone. "He'll get over it," I said aloud to myself.

<u>Ch. 6</u>

Streetz

Like A Moth To A Flame

The silence in the car was killing me. Sin was still pissed about the radio incident the other day. I could see she was just as stubborn as Belle. "You're back on this shit again? Come on ma…. You really thought I would put you out?" I playfully mushed her head. She looked at me and rolled her eyes. She could play this lil mad shit all she wanted. I don't know though, maybe I shouldn't have been so harsh with her. I know how delicate her lil ass could be. "That was so uncalled for. I swear, you're like a big ass kid." She said looking out the window.

"So, you grown then? Lil Sinclaire's not a kid anymore. Is that what you're saying?" I laughed and she punched me in the arm. When we pulled up to the school, I said, "I got a couple of stops to make today, so I'll be a little late picking you up." She stepped out of the car saying under her breath, "What else is new." She slammed the door and stomped her way into the school. I had bigger fish to fry, I'd deal with her and that temper later. I text JT and Marcus letting them know I was outside. This was my favorite part of the game. I loved to get my hands dirty. It was always some rookies trying to show a mufucka up. When all was said, and done, the streets were gonna feel me.

"I'm telling you, that man won't have his trap in the same spot. If he does, he's a stupid mufucka," Marcus said. JT felt differently. "Nah man, if business was good for him there, I don't think he would. Especially since he's new in town." I was quiet as I drove to Big D's. I knew he wouldn't be there also, but to appease JT, I went anyway. JT was the type, he had to be proved wrong. Once we drove by and saw that the house was a ghost spot, I looked at JT and said. "You happy now? Let's get to plan B."

I pulled out my cell and called my cousin Teetee. I knew she was still fucking wit D, so I had her agree to hit that nigga up for me. "Aaaah yeah, Hello," I laughed. She had him right where I wanted him. "The back door unlocked?" I whispered. "Ooo shit, don't stop, Yeaaaa." I clicked the line. We parked in the backyard and crept our way through the back door. We could hear them in the front bedroom. When I spotted the niggas clothes on the living room floor, I emptied his pockets. Now I knew he was in there unarmed and broke. What a dumb ass nigga. He just moved out here not even two months ago, and he trusting bitches like that? I shook my head laughing and tossed the money and the burner to Marcus.

I crept in the room, and watched as Big D was sweating and blowing my cousin Teetee's back out. The sight alone made me wanna burn a hole in this nigga. I placed the pistol to his dome and pulled the hammer back. He froze on contact. I nodded to Teetee. She jumped up and hurried out of the room. "And put some fuckin clothes on girl," I said, still heated that she was fucking.

She was legal at eighteen, but she would always be my baby cousin. I would have to shake those images out of my dome, or every time I saw her I would go upside her head.

"Well, well, well. You didn't think I would just let that shit from the other night fly, did you?" I could hear him cussing under his breath. By now, he knew he had fucked up. "I just gotta ask bruh. What made you think you could trust a bitch you been fuckin for a month, in a city you don't even know?" Marcus and JT laughed. I didn't find the shit funny. If anything, it was sad. "My nigga, we savages round here. You underestimated your opponent and that cost you," I cracked him in the head with the burner. Once he was out cold, JT and Marcus wrapped him in the bedsheets and walked him out to the car. "Yo Tee, let's go over this again. Anybody ask you if you've seen D, you ain't seen him since yall broke up a month ago. We got the nigga car, so don't worry about it. I just need you to keep your story straight, Aight?" She was now dressed in her robe. She shrugged and said, "Yeah, yeah, just don't forget to run me my bread." Since birth her ass has always been about a dollar. I laughed and handed her a stack. "You'll get the rest once everything's taken care of."

I had JT and Marcus take my car, and I drove Big D's Charger. We met up at the spot. It was our personal stash spot. An old abandoned warehouse with a basement. We had no use for the basement until today. After chaining him up and stringing him to the pole in the center of the room. I turned to Marcus and JT, "I got a couple runs to make. What ya'll wanna do? Wait it out until he wakes up, or just come back and handle this shit later." Marcus shrugged and JT said, "As tight as those chains are, he won't be going anywhere. Let me just gag his mouth so he won't go hollin and bringing unwanted attention." I said, "Good thinking bro."

We already had agreed to use the school as an alibi. That way if anything comes up, the school covered our tracks. I noticed Sin sitting outside so I told the guys I'd catch them later. "Don't go getting off track my nigga, you know we got biz to take care of." Marcus said. He was always peeping shit. He could see me watching Sin from the corner of my eye. "Bruh, I'm on it. No need to worry about me, aight? When class lets out, we'll head back over." He shrugged as he dapped me up and went inside.

As I made my way over to the bench Sinclaire was sitting on, I noticed she was reading a book called The Juice Box by Kali2cute. It must be good because she was so into it, she didn't notice me sit down beside her. She continues to read and eventually I say, "Yawl girls something else." She looked up and said, "What do you mean?" I shook my head and said, " If you know you got a good nigga, who been faithful to yo ass since yawl first got together, Why yawl still don't trust em?" She gave me a look that said, Nigga Please "A woman's intuition never lies T. You had to have given her some reason to question your relationship." I knew I had to come at shawty different in order to get her trust. I could tell she was a good girl. "I swear man, I hadn't cheated on her until she started constantly arguing about me cheating. Now we broke up, and she bout to have the baby. I don't know what I should do." I was laying it on pretty thick, but shit, fuck it. "You're having another baby?" she asked in shock. I nodded and said, "Yeah, she just found out the other day. Shit, and now she decides she wanna break up with me." I said. "Damn, I thought yawl lived together?" she said. "Nah, I stay with my folks." Ok, so we aren't really broken up, and yes, I still stay there, but I knew she wouldn't give me the time of day if she knew. A little white lie wouldn't hurt.

"Are you staying for the rest of class?" She said getting up to head back inside. "Yeah, I'm staying. You going to your aunt's house again?" She nodded. When she got up, I couldn't help staring at her from behind. "Yo T," I turned around and noticed our instructor James walking towards me. I could tell from the look on his face, he saw me watching Sinclaire. "Watch ya self playa. Don't get yourself involved in something you can't get out of." James knew all about my girl Belle and our kid. He knew I was trying to be a family man. "She's trying to stay focused. With you whispering lies in her ear, she won't get too far." I shook my head. I knew he was right, but it was something about her. It was hard to leave her alone.

****

When I pulled up to Sin's aunts house, I looked over at Sinclaire. She wasn't quick to get out, so I knew she was ready to talk about something. "Wassup ma," she looked out the window and back at me. "I can tell when your stressing T, What's up with you?" I didn't wanna involve her in my bullshit. I had been stressing all day about how I would handle the Big D situation. I gotta start working on my poker face, too many mufuckas reading me. "Don't worry about that, I'm good, just got a lot on my mind." I shook my head. She grabbed my face and turned my attention back to her. "Don't get caught up in this street shit, it's not worth it. Yes, the money's good. Yes, the bills are paid, … but to leave your kids alone in a world like this isn't worth it."

When I couldn't stand to look her in the eye and lie, I turned my head and said, "I know what I'm doing bruh. Don't worry about me. I'm good." She rolled her eyes, and got out of the car. Before walking inside, she turned back and said, "You're so fucking stubborn. The moment you became a father, it was no longer all about you. That's all I'm saying." When I noticed she was safe inside, I pulled off.

Putting my focus back on the business at hand, I headed back to the school to pick up Marcus and JT. I decided I would off the nigga, slowly. Rule number one was always no mercy. He decided his fate the day he shot at me and my boy. I had done my research on Big D too. I wanted to make sure all my bases were covered. I needed to know who all his associates were, here in Gulfport, and in New York, his hometown. He thought he had secured his families whereabouts, but a few hours with my boy Lance, and his homeys were singing like Kelly Price.

Once the boys and I had returned to the warehouse, we noticed Big D was still standing tall. He was a hard one to crack under pressure. I slowly walked up on him. Snatching the hoodie from his face, I looked him in his eyes. There really wasn't much to say, I was beyond the point of forgiveness. As bad as Big D claimed to be and tried to stand tall, his weakness would always find a way out. This mufucka had pissed his pants. The strong stench had given him away. I looked at Marcus and said, "I know you smell this pissy ass nigga." I looked back at D and said, "I would hose yo ass down, but it'd be a waste of my time. I don't like to waste time, feel me?" That was what broke the camels' back. He knew his last moments were being counted down. Once he started whining and crying, I pulled the rag out of his mouth. "Listen man, If it's money you want, I have plenty. You don't have to do this. I got kids fam,"

"You should've thought about that shit before you tried to gun me and my nigga down. I took that shit personal bruh. What about you J? You took it personal too uh?" JT just mugged, answering my question with his posture. My nigga was thirty-eight hot. I knew if it was up to him, ole boy would be knee deep in his grave right now. My clothes had started to stick to my body, so I knew it was about time we wrapped things up. Grabbing the 380 from my back strap, I said a prayer to myself. I knew once I pulled the trigger, there would be no coming back. I had never taken a life before. Shit, I never thought it would ever come to it. Now here I am, face to face with a man who tried to silence mine. One thing my brother Trell taught me, was to never leave open wounds. "Whatever you start, you gotta finish." I thought to myself as I pulled the trigger.

<u>Ch. 7</u>

Sin

Emotional Rollercoaster

As soon as I got into the car, I could tell something was wrong. I didn't want to pry, so I kept my thoughts to myself. He was unusually quiet. Sometimes I just didn't get him. He'd just go into this zone. When I couldn't take the awkwardness anymore, I broke the ice asking, "Where are we going? Don't tell me we're going to be late again." He just continued to ride and stare out the window. "Fine, Ignorance is bliss I guess," I said sarcastically.

We pulled up to a nice sized average home. It had an old aura about it. I knew this had to be his grandmother's house. He told me he was living with her while he got his money right. When we got inside I took a seat on the couch. I was surprised at how neat he kept the place. Even his bedroom was spotless. I could tell he had a lot of respect for her. Seeing this side of him had turned me on in the worst way. I knew he didn't see me that way, so I never spoke of my inner thoughts. As we were heading out to the car, he asked me did I want some potato chips. There he goes with that caring shit. Now why is he thinking of my stomach when he's obviously upset about something. Could he like me? I don't know All sorts of thoughts were running through my mind.

During class once we got back to school, he was all I could think about. I was supposed to be studying for my big test and all I could think about was how soft his lips would feel. During break, me and the girls were all laughing about last night's episode of "Who do you love?" when he stopped at our table. "Wassup, I wanna laugh too," He just had to be the center of attention. I was too done with his goofy ass. As the girls began to fill him in on the show, I just laughed and ignored him. I could tell he didn't like that, cuz he knew I had a little crush on him. I don't know why he likes to play with my emotions and shit, when he knows he doesn't like me like that.

I couldn't take all the girls flirting with him, so I decided to go outside for the rest of break. He had followed me out there, which didn't surprise me. "I thought ya'll were having a pretty deep conversation? What are you running behind me for?" I laughed and leaned on the hood of a car. He stood in front of me and said, "I don't know why you playing games and shit. You need to get wit this money train girl," He laughed and I laughed right along with him, because he knew he was nowhere near a money train right now. He was still in his early stages of selling. Nowhere near the big boy money. He stopped laughing and said, "Bitch, it wasn't that funny. You laughing a lil too hard nigga," I was dying laughing. He could be so funny when he wanted to be.

"I gotta make a couple stops before I drop you off. That's cool?" he said sitting next to me on the hood of the car. "Gotdamn Tommy, every day you always making me late. If my mom get to trippin, I swear I'm

cussin you out tomorrow bruh." He didn't reply. I
looked down at my phone to check the time and it was
well past our break. I grabbed his arm pulling him
towards the door. "Already getting me cussed out by
Mr. James, You know he finna snap my head off." We
laughed heading back into class.

"Look at ya bighead ass walking in all late and shit. I told
yawl fifteen minutes. How you get forty five out of
fifteen minutes?" James was not playing. The rest of my
small class was standing around the craps table
practicing double stacking and I was the only one late. I
was so embarrassed. My cousin Kelly began snickering
once I stood next to her. I kicked her under the table.
"Everything's all fun and games until it's time to see
who gon ace this test bitch," Kelly smirked. We had
made a little wager on who would make the better
grade. We were always challenging each other like that.
We're practically best friends. "If you two don't pay
attention, Ya asses will be out my class." James said
shooting the first dice of the day.

****

A few hours after being dropped off at home, I was
fighting with my sister. Once again, she didn't know
how to keep her hands off other people's things. "You
got one more time lil gul. I'm not gon keep fighting wit
you about my stuff. Next time, I'm goin upside ya
head." She laughed and threw my clothes on the floor. I
slapped her before they even hit the ground. We
started fighting and I could hear my mom in her room.
"Don't make me come in there. I'm in the middle of

Grey's Anatomy, so both of yall asses will be whooped. Play wit me if ya want to." As I had Latavia in the headlock, and she was pulling my hair, we both heard my mom's footsteps at the same time. I rushed back into my room, and Lala ran into hers. My mom did not play, she had long passed the point of using belts on us.

As I sat in my room, my mind became filled with thoughts of Tommy. I knew he was out handling business, but I just wanted to check in with him. I always did the opposite of what he asked me anyway, I laughed to myself as I picked up the phone to call him. "Didn't I tell you not to call me, I'll call you," he said. "Yes, but I was just trynna ask you about something." He didn't know it, but Tommy had opened a can of emotions once he had asked me about my personal life. I felt like I could talk to him about my personal life also. "I'll call you back, ". Shit, I was only used to dealing with guys who could sit around all day and talk to me when I wanted. I wasn't used to one being unavailable to me. Especially since he claimed he wasn't with his baby moms right now. I called him back, "Bruh, you buggin. Wassup?" I laughed and said, "Nothing, why something gotta be up, "He laughed and said, "What you trynna do, cuz you ain't callin me just to talk," I was put on the spot. All I knew was every time I spoke to him, I just wanted to be around him. Whenever I rode with him, I didn't wanna get out the car. It was clear to me, that I was craving him in a way, I had never experienced. When I couldn't think of how to answer him, I said, "What you wanna do?" he said, "We ain't got nothin to talk about if you ain't suckin," I looked at the phone crazy, "Boy bye, you trippin," I hung up the phone seething. How dare he? I jumped up from the bed and began pacing my bedroom. All kinds of thoughts went through my head. "Who does he think he is? I only do that for guys I love. Does he really think I'm that type of chic? I bet he's bluffing tho, ..." I said aloud to myself. I knew he was trynna play me, so I said Ok, since he wanna play.... Lets play ball then, I called him back, "Ok.... I'll do it." He sounded shocked when he said, "You gon suck me up?" Just hearing him say it had me trippin out, but it wouldn't be my first time. "Yeah, if I can get it after." "I'll be there in fifteen."

I asked my mom if I can run to the store with my friend. She didn't mind, so when he called back and said he was outside, I took three deep breaths and left. He brought me to his secret place. I was comfortable anywhere with him. He seemed to take any butterflies I had in my gut before, away. When he pulled it out and looked at me to see if I would really do it, I showed him, he wasn't working with a little girl. Even though, technically I was. I had never made love to a man. I usually had sex because it was what was required of me. No man had ever cared about my wants and needs. I pulled him into my mouth and noticed he was a lot bigger than I expected. I think he was more turned on by the fact that I was actually doing it. He probably thought I was a virgin.

As I lay back on the couch, I noticed him put the condom on, I had a clear view of him in the night. My eyes bucked at the reality of the situation. This nigga would break my walls. I had always heard how the girls would say, "That bitch ain't got no walls," I started to tell him I couldn't do it, but he had already pushed in. I winced in pain, He stopped and asked me, "Are you okay?" I nodded yes, but inside I was hurting. He went deeper and I cried a little. When he went even deeper, and I couldn't take the pain any longer, a sensation I had never felt before took over me. I moaned from deep within my throat. My hands began to roam his back, and he made me feel alive for the first time. We picked up a steady rhythm, and nothing else in that moment mattered.

<u>**Ch. 8**</u>

Ron

Caught Up

"Two detectives in Gulfport will be waiting for you as soon as you enter their city limits. I want you to call them as soon as you get there. If it takes them too long to hear from you, they will come get you and detain you. Then I will be forced to come down there. You don't want me to come down, Do you Ronte?" Detective Daniel Foreman was a hard, body building prick from Jackson, MS. "Nah, it's all good." I said just to shut his ass up. I couldn't believe I had gotten caught up in this shit. Everybody knows, Snitches get stiches. So how the hell is this happening right now. I knew I should've just took my time like a G. Thinking about that ten year stretch though, had a nigga reconsidering.

"I've been trailing this punk for the last two years trying to catch him. Who knew I would luck up on a friend of his." I rolled my eyes and said, "How many times I gotta tell you, we ain't friends. I just met the nigga like a week or two ago. You trippin bruh. I fuck wit his homey, I don't even know that man." I couldn't help but wonder what Streetz had done for him to have such a hard-on for him.

I got caught up last night. The narcs pulled me over with two bricks in the trunk. I knew I was done for when they brought me in to the station. If I wasn't so jealous of Streetz friendship with Donte, I probably would have thought twice about taking the nigga down. Once I was cornered in the room and they told me how they had been watching me and my boys for the last few weeks, I knew this had nothing to do with me. They were looking for someone, in particular.

As soon as they brought me in, they threw Streetz picture down in front of me. "Tommy Mills aka Streetz. This is who we want. If you work with me to get him, we'll cut your time in half." I looked at this bald head mufucka and said, "Do I look stupid to you? I already know what this is. If I give anybody up, I want a clean slate." He said, "Well that would require your full cooperation. That means wires, phone tap, the whole nine. Are you ready for that? You think you can handle that?" I didn't want any part of this shit, but what choice did I have? "Yeah, I'm down."

When they found out I would be moving to Gulfport, MS in a few days, they came up with a plan. I was to become an informant. Every meeting Tommy and I had, I would be wired. My phone would always be tapped so that any conversation with him would be on record. They were determined to catch him slipping. I went home to finish packing. Looked like I'll be moving sooner than I thought.

"You be careful down there Ron. I told Gina to keep a close eye on you. I know how you like to stay in trouble." Moms wasn't ready to see me go, but she knew I had to take care of business. She did the best she could with her job cleaning houses, but it wasn't enough money to raise three kids on. I had to step up and be a man. "Ma, I'm good. I don't know why you told Teetee to look out for a nigga, when you know she down there trying to get to the paper her damn self. How many jobs she got now, three?" I laughed. My mom laughed along with me because she knew I was right. Hearing my twin baby sisters running down the hall, I scooped them up to say goodbye. "You leavin RaRa?" that was their nickname for me. "Yea, Rara's gotta go for a little while boo. I'll be back though. I want yawl to take care of mommy while I'm gone ok? Be good lil girls for her," They gave me a big kiss and ran back into their room. As my mom packed the last of my clothes, I could tell she wanted to cry. I didn't have time for emotions. "Come on Ma, dang, You act like I'll be gone for good. I'll just be down there for the school year." She sniffed and said, "I'm just used to having you close. I know this is the best move for you right now, but It's just gonna take some getting used to, that's all," My mom was so soft spoken I hardly heard her speak. I hugged her and let her cry on my chest. I whispered, "I love you too ma."

****

When I made it to Gulfport, I followed Daniels orders and reported to the station. I tried to keep my identity concealed by wearing shades and a hat. They introduced me to an officer named Nate Parker. He was a skinny dark cat with glasses. He informed me that he was who I report to every week. Sort of like a parole officer. If anyone asked, that's what I was to tell them. I hated everything about this, but I knew it was either his life or mine. Once I finished my meeting with Parker, I called Donte to let him know I was here.

"Call ya boy up. I'm headed to my aunt's crib first, unpack and shit. Then I'll be on my way to the school. Oh yeah, and tell him to text me the address." "Gotcha," My aunt had called me earlier, letting me know she'd be at work by the time I made it in. She said for me to make myself at home, but all I wanted to do was drop my stuff off and hit the streets. Gulfport had an entirely different vibe from Jackson. I loved the beach the most. From the palm trees and heavy traffic to the big casinos. I may never go back home I laughed to myself.

Once I made it to the school, class was already in session. I didn't know who I was supposed to speak to about enrolling, so I just went into the first office I saw. "How may I help you?" A lovely wide eyed, caramel beauty asked me. "I'm here to enroll. My friend said he spoke to someone about me. Tommy Mills?" She smiled and said, "Yes, we were notified about your arrival. Do you have your high school diploma or GED?" I nodded and said, "I don't have any of my paperwork. I graduated, but I didn't walk the stage to receive my diploma." She stood and went into one of her file cabinets. I couldn't help staring as she walked. "That won't be a problem, we'll just contact your last school and have them fax over your documents. What's the name of the school?" As she sat back down our eyes connected. I noticed her breath catch. She hurriedly looked back down at her paperwork.

"Jackson Heights High School. What's your name Beautiful?" Taken off-guard, she paused, then replied, "My name is Alexandria Whitfield, but you sir, will call me Mrs. Whitfield. I'll be your academy advisor." She made sure to expose her ring finger to my attention. I was one who loved a challenge. I'll play this little game with her for now, but let's see how long she can keep it up.

Once we were finished with my paperwork, she took me on a tour of the campus. The setup was dope. It seemed like a pretty chill place to attend. It was very different from an ordinary school. She made sure to stress the rules of the campus. I guess she figured I would be trouble. I don't know where she got that idea. I noticed a shorty eyeing me down at the table out back. I winked at her. She smiled and started giggling with her friends. At least I had a shorty to spend a little time with while I'm here.

"You will start on Monday. Each month you'll receive a stipend for two hundred dollars, plus your two-hundred-dollar lunch card. Do you have any more questions for me Mr. Smith?" She said as we ended the tour. "No ma'am. It was a pleasure meeting you Mrs. Whitfield. I look forward to Monday." I said with a wink. She turned back into her office. As I walked out to my car, I noticed shorty from earlier arguing with her guy. He shoved her and got into his car. "I don't have a ride home Gerald. What the fuck is your problem?" she yelled. He flipped her the finger and drove off. I just shook my head.

"Come on shorty, you ain't gotta put up wit that shit. Fuck that nigga." She turned with a scowl. "You would be the one to witness that." She said wiping her eyes. I laughed and told her to hop in. "Whose car is this? I know it ain't yours." She said, admiring my new maxima. My mom bought it for me as a graduation gift.

"Just give me your address so I can GPS it. You're worrying about the wrong thing boo," she ran off her address with an attitude. This was gonna be a long ride.

"How you invite me down here bruh, and you ain't nowhere in sight." I could hear Tommy laughing in the phone. "I only keep my credits together so I can get that check playboy. I be in and out." I laughed while pulling out of the school. Noticing shorty fixing her makeup in the mirror, I spoke to Tommy in code. "So, when are we getting up so I can put in that work? You know how I get down." "I'll text you my address. Meet me in an hour. I got ya," "Ok coo, I'm droppin off this shorty from the school, so I should make it there in time." He laughed and said, "Which one?" I looked over at shorty and realized I hadn't gotten her name. "I call her Honey Caramel," She rolled her eyes, and said, "My name is Kelly," I said, "Kelly?" sucking his teeth, Tommy said, "Ahh hell nah. Yo, hit me back when you drop that bird bitch off," "Well damn, I got you woe," As soon as I hung up the phone, shorty went in. "Yo, Who the fuck was that? Talking all that shit, I'll show him a fucking bird bitch." "Calm down shorty, that was my mans from school. He's the reason I'm starting Monday. I'm from Jackson." I said trying to calm her crazy ass down. She flipped her hair and said, "Oh, you sure didn't say anything to defend me nigga," rolling my eyes, I put my attention back on the road.

When we pulled up to her spot, I was more than happy to get her out of my car. Tommy was right, Kelly was a bird bitch. We argued the whole ride. She wouldn't stop touching all my shit. Going through my glove compartment. Yapping about her different dudes. The shit was annoying. "You think you can help me out wit something real quick?" I looked at her skeptically. "Depends on what it is," she smiled and said, "Boy, quit playing. It's just I have this leak in my sink and I was wondering if you could take a look at it real quick," I quickly shook my head and said, "Nah, I can't help ya boo. You heard me on the phone, I gotta go meet my homey." As soon as I started the car to let her know I was serious, she rubbed my crotch and said, "I'm sure they wouldn't mind if you're a few minutes late," I licked my lips and said, "I guess he can wait a minute or two." I hopped out, shaking my head as I followed her inside.

Sin

Free

For some reason, I found myself looking for him every day in class. Waiting on his arrival. Even though we rode together every day, he often ditched class and made it back before class was over to bring me home. Which was thoughtful of him. As I sat daydreaming about Tommy in the courtyard, my cousin Kelly walked over and sat next to me. I was so distracted, I didn't notice. She nudged me. "Did you hear me girl?" I shook my head no. "I said, have you met Ron?" I rolled my eyes, "No, who's Ron?" I just knew she was about to tell me about another one of her flings. I keep trying to tell her, it wasn't always about a man's wallet. Hell, I need to be taking my own advice. Our motto has always been, M.O.N. (Money Over Niggas) but growing up, I've realized you can't always be about the almighty dollar. That's how a lot of lives were lost.

"Ron is the new guy from Jack town. He fucks wit Tommy and his crew. Girl he was so fine, I had to try that nigga out." Kelly said. I laughed while shaking my head. "Uh uh, now you know you shouldn't be fucking wit these niggas at school. If anything were to pop off, you fucking up the bag sis," She shrugged and said, "Girl, he is the bag. I saw the niggas pockets were laced. Plus, he's pushing a Maxima. I know he got bread." Why is she always clocking mufuckas pockets? I couldn't help laughing at her stupid ass. She swung her hair and did the milly rock. "I am not about to play with you today Kelly," I laughed walking back inside. Kelly came up behind me.

When Kelly pointed Ron out to me, I smirked. I already knew how this would play out. As soon as I noticed him, I could tell he was a scrub. Everything about his persona screamed, wanna be player. I could see how he and Tommy were friends. Most of his friends were scrubs. JT is the only one who seems like he's got a bit of sense. I watched as Kelly walked over to him attempting to kiss him. He side stepped her. I snapped my head about to go off, when Kelly told me to chill. "What you mean chill? He just completely ignored you," I was even more upset at how cool and calm Kelly was being. She claimed ole boy was her dude. "He just doesn't like public affection. I get it. Why you trippin though? If I'm cool with it, you should be good." I threw my hands up in frustration and walked away before I said something that would damage our friendship.

Sometimes I didn't understand Kelly. Why she chose the dead-beat guys as her boyfriends, I couldn't tell you. There were plenty of good guys who have been trying to get her attention for years, but she's never paid them any mind. We would attend parties together and she would leave with the idiot groping her on the dancefloor. I knew she could be pretty thottish, but enough was enough. She had three kids at home she needed to be concerned about. They need a dad in their life. Every weekend she was either in some new mans bed, or in some club, shutting down the bar. After figuring she'll never change, I realized I just had to keep my distance.

By the time Tommy had arrived back to the school, class had let out. We were all standing in the courtyard. "Come on, I got a few more stops to make." He said opening the passenger side door for me. He was dressed in a white dress shirt with black pants. He must have gotten an audition from one of the casinos. "How'd you score an audition before graduation? You still have three months left of school." I was impressed. He started up the car and said, "Shit, with my skills, James was able to hook it up for me. I gotta drive out to the bay. That's the only fucked up part about it." By the bay, he meant Bay St. Louis. It was the next town over. I was a little sad, because that meant, I may not be able to see him tonight. When he dropped me off, he made little contact, as if he was pulling away from me. I tried not to let it get to me, but my feelings had gotten involved.

****

I was in the middle of cleaning my room, when my mom called me into the living room. "Yes ma'am?" She was folding clothes and wanted me to put them up for her. I had a soft spot for my mom. She had sacrificed so much for my sister and me. I've just always wanted to make her happy. With our relationship on the rocks, sometimes I didn't know whether her hardness toward me was coming from a place of love, or anger. I knew sometimes she treated me bad, because of her anger towards my dad. I had only met him twice in my life. When he abandoned us when I was born, my mom did what she had to do to take care of me. It wasn't until my sister came along that things changed. To watch my sister, get the love she needed from her dad every day, was hard. I would rebel sometimes, only because I felt unwanted a lot. I didn't mean to take it out on the people who loved me.

"Ma, was Peter the first man you ever loved?" She raised an eyebrow and said, "No, why do you ask that Sinclaire?" Peter was my mom's husband and Latavia's dad. My mom could always read when I thought I liked a guy. "I'm just asking. So, who was your first love ma? And why did yawl break up?" she shook her head and went back to folding clothes. I came and sat next to her. "I'm serious ma. I just wanna know," after taking what seemed like a century she finally replied. "His name was George. We were high school sweethearts. His sophomore year, he was captain of the basketball team. He was tall, dark and handsome. He gave me the worst butterflies girl," she laughed and took a breath. "We had been together for three years. I just knew we were going to get married. While we were going through our school ups and downs, his parents were also. They went through a nasty divorce, and when the dust settled, George ended up moving with his mom to another state. That was the last I had heard of him." Seeing my mom's expressions change, I could tell she still loved him. I don't know why I even brought it up. "I'm sorry ma, I didn't know you still cared about him," She sniffed and said, "Girl please, I'm a married woman now. Ain't nobody thinking about George. Peter is all the man I need. I see you have a new boo though, that's the only time you ask about men. Now, spill it." She said. I laughed and said, "I don't know, we're not really together, but I really like him though." She said, "Well why aren't yawl together?" I looked down at my hands. She repeated her question and I said, "We've just been friends, and neither of us has said anything about being together," My mom laughed and said, "He must be with someone," I shook my head no, "I mean, he has a baby mom, but he says they're not together though," "Have you been to his house?" "Yes ma'am. He's been living with his granny. I'm not even sure if he likes me the way I like him," "Well who is he?" Again, I looked down at my hands. "Sinclaire Laverne Evans, I raised you to speak your mind, why do you keep looking at your hands. I'm up here girl," I didn't know what I should say. If I told her who it was, she wouldn't allow me to be friends with him anymore. Especially because of his type of lifestyle. She's met him a couple of times already. I decided to go with my gut answer. "His name's Rico. He lives over on Rich. I met him the other day at Kelly's party." The lie flew out of my mouth so quickly, I hadn't realized I'd said it. She pursed her lips and said, "Um hmm. I guess I'll have to meet this Mr. Rico. Who's some of his people?" I let out the biggest breath, as I made up this imaginary man I had fallen for.

When I made it back to my room, I had missed several phone calls. I had forgotten to turn the ringer back on. I always turned the ringer off at night so that my mom wouldn't hear me sneaking on the phone. Yes, I was nineteen, with a curfew and phone laws in my mom's house. When I checked the calls, I noticed they were all from Tommy. I could already hear him cursing me out. He was very impatient. Sometimes I couldn't stand his stalker-ish ways. Other times, it was a huge turn on.

As soon as he picked up, I said, "My bad, I had the ringer off. Wassup?" he asked, "Can you get out?" I knew it would be a stretch, but I said, "Yeah, give me an hour though, cuz my mom's in the living room." He said bet, and hung up. I just didn't understand how whenever he called, I would risk it all to see him. It's like my body had a mind of its own. When I was sure my mom was sleep, I called him back and snuck out of the back door.

***

As the wind was blowing through my hair, I was trying hard to keep my heart from beating out of my chest. We sat in complete silence. It was a comfortable silence. He always made me feel so at ease, as if I could ride with him to the end of the world and back. I didn't know what it was about him, but I was loving every minute of finding out. When I noticed he stopped in the middle of a vacant wooded area, I looked at him confused. "Why are we out here?" He took my hand and said, "Just chill wit me, talk wit me. What's on your mind?" I sat back in my seat and said, "I mean, to be honest, You. I've been worried about you." He went quiet again. I knew whatever it was, he didn't want to talk to me about it, but I wouldn't give up that easily.

"You don't have to tell me what happened, but I just need to know you're ok." I didn't know if it was because of our intimate contact that we've shared, or because of these new feelings I was feeling for him, but I began to think about his well-being as much as I thought of my own.

Instead of answering my question, he began rubbing my hand. The electricity from his touch, had shocked my body. I watched as he thwittled with my thumb. My breathing had slowed and my breath became shallow. I didn't know what he was doing to me, but I never wanted it to end. He brought out the woman in me. I felt free to be myself with him. I discovered this sexual appetite, I never knew existed with a man. I reached over and began to unbutton his pants. As I took him into my mouth, I treated him as if he were my very own popsicle and I was enjoying my favorite flavor. When I knew he was coming to an end, he lifted my head and said, "Let's get in the back," I had no complaints as I joined him.

The fact that we were in the backseat of his car, and at any moment we could be stopped by law enforcement, seemed to heighten the mood. We were wide open and free for the world to see. I knew in the morning I would think I had lost my mind, but right now, I was enjoying the moment. He seemed in a rush to get things started and I halt him by saying kind of bossily, "Hold on, ... Let me relax," I take a second to adjust myself in his arms, then look up into his eyes and say, "Ok, ...I'm ready."
At that moment, I gave myself completely to him. I trusted him with everything in me. He felt it too. When

he entered me, I felt like he opened another door inside me. It was indescribable. My mind just went to a whole other region. He was so careful with me, it was something I had never experienced before. I knew from that moment on, my love would never belong to another.

<u>Ch. 10</u>

Streetz

In Too Deep

I had just left one of my jump-offs spot. She had a package for me. I hit her off pretty decent. Since hooking up with Sinclaire a week ago, I've been avoiding her. Most days, I wouldn't even come to class. Shit I had broken my number one rule, never show feelings. We were no longer having sex, we were making love. As much as my mind told me to cut shorty loose, I could feel myself getting in too deep. This was supposed to only be me getting some extra business from her people. It's gotten out of hand now. She would call me all throughout the day, and Belle had started looking at me with suspicion in her eyes. I knew if I didn't get my act together, shit would hit the fan.

I met up with Ron at one of our spots around town. I was gonna test him out, to see how solid he really was. "What's good Woe?" I said getting out of my car. I don't know why this tall mufucka didn't play basketball. He would go pro for sure. "What's good? You got that work for me?" he said. For some reason he seemed kind of antsy. I'm guessing he was just eager to show off. "Hell yeah, but we'll get to that shit in a minute. Tell me what you fucking wit that bird bitch Kelly for? How the fuck that shit happen?" I said laughing. I didn't have to ask how it happened. Everyone knew Kelly was going. If a nigga looked like he had that bread, she was going. "My nigga, the bitch was practically throwing the pussy at me bruh," I laughed and said, "Hell nah, you fell for the okie doke my dude. You in there now, might as well set up shop wit her,"

Homey wasn't having that, he said, "Fuck no. She gave me dome when I brought her home the other day, and I piped her down, but shit, I got my eye on lil mama in the office though," I shook my head, "Ooowee, I know you ain't talking bout the married broad wit the fat ass. That's a tough one yo, I been trying to get that since I first started." He laughed and said, "Hell I'm damn near in there. I'm wearing her ass down. I can tell she feeling me." I laughed, shook my head and said, "Good luck with that. Just watch out for that loud mouth bitch Kelly though. That's a hood bitch for real." Once we finished chopping it up, we handled business. I let Ron get off a couple bags of weed. I wanted to see how quickly he could get his clientele up, down here.

"Once you're done, I'll know where we stand my friend." I said. Ron dapped me up and we made plans to meet back up tomorrow at the same time. When I hopped back in my ride, I noticed I had missed five calls from Belle. "Damn," I said to myself. I had forgot I was supposed to take her and the baby to Walmart tonight. Since it was still early, hopefully she doesn't trip.

"Why do you have a phone if you're not gonna answer it? Anything could have been going on," Belle immediately went in on me. I knew it was coming so I just let her rant. Usually when she would rant, she'd start to bring up old shit. Silence was the best response. I just picked Kalashia up and buckled her into her car seat. Eventually when she realized, I wasn't gonna argue, she got into the car, fuming on the inside. As we rode in silence, I thought of how strained Belle and I's relationship was. Things had become so tense between us. At night, we slept more like roommates than lovers. I had to fix things. With a new baby on the way, all I needed was more drama in the home.

When we made it to Walmart, Belle had softened up a bit. We spent most of our time chasing Kalashia in the toy section. Every time Belle told her no about something, I would come behind her and buy it anyway. She was a daddy's girl. One tear and I was a goner. I wanted my children to have the best. I loved to spoil them, Belle included. Even with her angry with me, I managed to put a smile on her face when I bought her a diamond pendant necklace.

As we neared the checkout line, Belle realized she had forgotten the box of baby food. "Babe, it's on the left side of the baby isle. The bottom row. Remember it says Gerber variety on the front." I shook my head and said, "I got it. We've been buying it long enough, I should know what the box looks like B," She laughed and started placing the items on the conveyor, while I rushed to the back.

I made it halfway to the baby section, and noticed Sinclaire laughing with her friend girl. She hadn't noticed me yet, so I sped up my pace. As soon as I thought I was in the clear, I heard, "Fancy running into you here, of all places." Damn "What's good boo?" I said hugging her while scoping my surroundings. She stepped back, looking me in my eyes. "I'm good, just wondering what's got you so jumpy?" I continued avoiding her eyes, because I knew I couldn't lie to her. "Oh nah, I'm straight. Just picking up some things for the baby. I'll hit you up later tho." As I walked off I could feel her burning a hole into my back. I knew she was mad. I'll cross that bridge when I get to it.

By the time I made it back to the register, Belle had everything packed in the buggy. She ignored me and continued out the door to the car. After paying for the baby food, I rush behind them. "What the fuck is wrong wit you?" I ask her as we put the food into the car. She ignores me and continues packing the groceries. "So that's what we doing now? Aight, bet."

Belle waited until Lashia was sleep before asking me about the girl in Walmart. Damn, I didn't think she saw me. I thought to myself. "That was a friend from school. She was asking me about the test this Friday." I said, hoping that would be the end of it. I guess I was wrong, "That's your fucking problem. You lie too damn much T. She had to have been more than a fucking friend the way yawl hugging each other and shit." I shook my head and said, "Belle, I told you, I know her from school. Chill the fuck out before you wake Lashia up." She wasn't trying to hear that, "I'm so fucking tired of the disrespect Tommy! When are you gonna grow the fuck up and realize you have a fucking family!" I was trying to keep myself calm because I knew going back and forth with her would upset the baby. "I'm not gonna argue with you B. That shit was nothing. You getting all riled up for nothing," She got quiet again. Too quiet. That was only the calm before the storm. "You know what? I can't do this shit anymore. I think you should stay with Nana for a while. I just need some space. This shit is unhealthy for me and the kids." Hell, I knew that was coming. This was our normal routine. I was always back and forth between Belle and Granny's. I didn't say anything the remainder of the ride.

Sin

Woman To Woman

"Are you sure it's supposed to look like this Temeka?" I ask fingering my curls. I've sat here for the last four hours getting my hair done, and I was not happy with the results. She popped her gum, and said, "Yes bitch, Ya hair is laid. Ladies, what yawl think of her hair?" I rolled my eyes. Mostly all the women said, "Yeah girl, it's cute." "That shit is tight," "Meka, do my hair like that next girl." I didn't care what they said, this shit was not cute. I wanted to ask for my money back, but it was only a dub, so I said Fuck it.

As I gathered my things to get ready to leave, I overheard a client sitting under the dryer talking with her friend. "Yes, girl. I finally got my revenge on that hoe. I told her the shit wasn't over." She laughed. Her friend said, "What you did girl?" "Shit, I didn't have to do much. I found out who her man was. The one always dropping her off in the Maxima," She smacked her lips and said, "Come to find out, my cousin Alex works at the nigga school. So, you already know I told Cuz to hop on him," Her friend started laughing. She said, "I know you ain't do Kelly like that Roxy," I knew I recognized that hoe when I walked in. Now it made since, her bitch ass was talking loud enough for me to hear, because she knew I would tell my cousin. You damn right I am, as soon as I figure out who the fuck Alex is.

I was so hot! I wanted to stomp a hole in that bitch. It's cool, I reminded myself that she would have to see me for it later. I called my mom to come pick me up, "I'm at work. Call someone to come get you. I had to work a double." I was frustrated but I didn't argue. I just said, "Yes ma'am," and hung up. I had called three of my relatives so far, and they were all busy. I refused to get stuck walking home again, so I called Tommy. "Hey, can I get a ride?" "Where from?" I told him the directions, and he said, "I'm in Biloxi right now boo. Why you ain't call me earlier?" I rolled my eyes and said, "I can wait on you to finish. I'm not in a rush, I just really need a ride home," "I won't be back on that side tonight Sin." I was instantly annoyed with him. He always put his business ahead of me. He's been acting funny lately too. Staying away from school so that he doesn't have to give me rides. Ignoring my calls. I don't know why I'm surprised. We've never made anything official between us. I can't expect him to make me wifey, when he has a baby mom he's been with for the last two years. I don't know why I deal with him anyway. I wish my body didn't crave him like it does. That would make things so much easier. Never the less, I would make sure I put a lot of distance between he and I in the future. Fuck that nigga

****

The next day in class, Mr. James was teaching us about the inside bets on the craps table. Now I could see why this was everyone's favorite game to bet. You could quadruple your bets in one game. A skilled player could become a millionaire overnight. When it came time for me to deal, I moved to stand behind the table, across from Mr. James holding the stick. Once everyone's bets were placed, Mr. James yelled, "No more bets." The shooter rolled the dice and it landed in the come line. I could hear Mr. James yell,

10 easy/hard 10.

Mark the 10.

Down behind the 10.

Field roll 10.

As I paid out the bets, and we repeated the process, I could feel myself relaxing more on the payouts. The more I dealt, the easier it became for me. I knew it would soon be a piece of cake. The shooter rolled again, this time the dice read eleven.

Yo 11 frontline winner 11.

Take the dont's.

Pay the line and field.

As soon as we paid everyone out, the bell rang for break. Kelly and I headed for the chow hall.

"No, Fuck that! I know she up here! Where the fuck is she Marcus?" We turned to see Marcus arguing with his baby mother at the front door. He was trying his hardest to calm her down. "Where is she? I'm not leaving until the bitch show her face! I know you fucking wit one of these hoes Marcus." I could feel Kelly nudging me in the side. I was too deep into the drama unfolding to notice. The girl yanked her arm from Marcus and stormed towards us. By this time, Kelly's nudges started to hurt, so I turned to her and said, "What bitch? Damn, that hurt." She turned me around and whispered, "Yo, if she asks us. We don't know Marcus aight?" I looked at her and shook my head. I swear, Kelly fucks with everybody's man. I'm always in some drama behind her ass. That's just how it is though. Family over Everything.

Once I turned back around, the girl was grilling us with her hands on her hips. "Yawl know Marcus?" We both shook our heads and said, "Nah," I said, "Shit, I be seeing him around the school from time to time, but I don't know him," She smirked and looked Kelly up and down. "Whatever, move out my way," Marcus had finally caught up to her and yelled while running behind her, "Baby wait, I told you I haven't been fucking wit nobody. You gone get me kicked out of school."

Kelly and I laughed as Marcus grabbed the girl up, carrying her back outside. I looked back at Kelly and said, "Bitch, how long you been fucking wit bowlegged Marcus?" She laughed and said, "He bowlegged for a reason," "Ew, Ya nasty." She said, "Ron been acting funny lately, so he's been my Mr. Fixit. If ya know what I mean," That's what I loved about her crazy ass, she kept me laughing. By the time we looked up at the clock, break was over. I told Kelly I would catch her later, I had to practice for this craps test.

As I walked over to the empty craps table, I noticed someone walk up behind me. When I turned around and noticed who it was, I turned back to my game and chose to ignore them. I had been playing silently for about fifteen minutes before he decided to speak. "So, you're really gonna do this huh?" I continue playing as if I didn't hear him. "Sin, what the fuck is your problem?" I roll my eyes and say, "I don't have a problem Tommy. What are you talking about?" I continue playing my game. Minding my own business. He takes the hint and walks off nodding his head. He turns and says, "Ok, that's how you want it." Shaking my head, I put my focus back on my game. I did not have time for the bull.

******

When I made it home, mom was in my ear yelling about me taking my driver's test again. "I mean it Sin. You have to get your license because this is ridiculous. I can't keep taking off work to come get you and your sister. You have a car waiting for you. You just have to get your license first. I'm not trying to fuss at you, but baby, you'll be twenty in January, and it's time for you to have your own car." Since I hadn't been riding home with Tommy anymore, it's been hard on my mom. She warned me before starting this school, that it would be hard for transportation. I didn't listen. I was too excited about joining. "Now, I'll take you when I have some off time. You just have to remind me," She said. I nodded and promised her I would.

My sister was in my room watching Martin. "Lala, why are you in my room?" I ask. She continues watching the screen as if she didn't hear me. I didn't feel like fighting her today, so I just got comfy on the bed next to her. We had a love/hate relationship. It was hard to explain. We always had each other's back. The bond we shared was unbreakable. I loved my mother and sister more than life itself. While watching tv, I heard the phone ring, when I looked to see who it was, I rolled my eyes and ignored the call. Latavia asked, "Why you ain't answer it?" I said, "Because it was for me, and I don't wanna talk to them." She laughed and said, "It must be that boy," I laughed. How the hell did she figure that out? "I see you sneak out all the time. I won't tell ma, but eventually she'll figure it out." I shook my head and said, "Girl, don't get caught up in these niggas man. Stay focused on school, cuz this shit is not worth the headache." We continue watching tv, as the phone continues to ring.

After an hour of torturing him, I finally decided to call him back. I said, "What Bruh? Don't be blowing me up and shit," What I didn't expect to hear was, "Who the fuck is this? And why are you calling my man?" I had to take a second to look at the phone before responding. I pointed for my sister to go in her room. Once she was gone, I said, "Put Tommy on the phone." I wasn't about to do this back and forth bullshit with her. "He's in the shower. Now, once again, who are you and why are you calling for my man?"

I laughed, hard as hell. "Bitch, if he's your man, keep his ass the fuck off my line. Matter fact, keep his ass out my fuckin face every day. He's annoying the fuck outta me." She laughed and said, "Ha, I know this ain't

that hoe from the school. Whoever you are bitch, I
don't have time for it today. He is my man, been that
for the last two years, and he ain't going nowhere." She
laughed and said, "You hoes kill me. Getting all in your
feelings about the next bitch man. When you need to
be concentrating on finding your own nigga." I shook
my head. If only this bitch knew how often she shares
her man. It's really sad. "I don't want ya man bitch, I just
can't seem to keep his ass away from me. Why don't
you do what the fuck you need to do at home, so he can
stop knocking at my door." I could hear Tommy in the
background, "Who dat?" she snapped at him and said,
"Whatever bird bitch you fuckin. You wonder why your
ass is still on Nana's fucking couch, cuz you ain't shit
nigga," I knew it was wrong, but I couldn't help
laughing. This was comedy at its best. I hung up on
them. I knew he would be calling me back tonight, but
fuck that shit. I'm done with his ass. I clearly remember
him telling me they were not together, on many
occasions. Ugh, why do guys lie so much?

<u>Ch. 12</u>

Streetz

Craving Your Body

I had just picked Ron up and we were now on our way back up to Jackson. We had to make another pick up. We were smoking a doobie and chatting about the bitches he was fucking wit from the school. "Yo, don't fuck wit that Shay bitch. You can do better than that. I ain't gon lie, she got a fat ass, but that bitch crazy." I said. Ron laughed and said, "Hell nah. I finally bagged ol girl though." I glanced his way to see if he was serious. He nodded. "How the hell you pull that off young blood? That bitch is married too," He laughed and said, "I know bruh, but one day she was wit it. She was like, 'What my man don't know won't hurt him.' We been getting it in ever since." I shook my head. "I gotta give it to you. If you bagged that? You's a bad mufucka." He passed me the joint and said, "Please believe me,"

"How you doin in BlackJack?" He shrugged and said, "It's straight. I got a while til I can catch up wit yo ass," I laughed and said, "It's not that hard bruh. As much as that nigga gets on my nerves, I have to give it to him, he's a good teacher." I was speaking about Mr. James. He's a retired casino dealer. He's spent twenty plus years in the industry. Everything I've learned, came from shadowing him. When I first got to the school, I was desperate for a good job. If slinging cards was

87

gonna do it for me, I was gonna be the best at it. That was my motto. "Yeah, that old man's crazy, but he can play though," As I passed Ron the doobie, I noticed one time a few cars behind me in my rearview. I quickly tossed the blunt out the window. Ron immediately looked shook. I looked at him crazy, "The fuck is wrong wit you? You gone make em pull us, the way you bitch'in up. Chill out bruh," I relaxed and continued driving the speed limit.

When they hopped behind us and flashed the lights, I knew this wasn't an ordinary stop. I mouthed to Ron as the officer walked toward my car, "Don't say nothing." I rolled my window down and said, "Hello officer, was I going over the speed limit sir? I was doing forty-five." I could turn on the charm when I had to. Don't let the street shit fool you, I was book smart also. We were lucky enough to be stopped by an asshole. "Would you mind stepping out of the vehicle with your hands in the air?" Damn I won't lie, at this point, I was getting nervous. I wondered why they needed to search my ride. Shit wasn't adding up. Ron and I got out and stood by as the officer searched the car. I knew I was clean, but depending on what type of officer he wanted to be today, this could play out any type of way. When he didn't find anything, he let us go. I finally let out the breath I had been holding.

I had been very careful on my route to and from Jackson every month. This didn't sit well with me at all. I was in another zone as we rode the rest of the way to Jackson. For them to stop me and immediately search my ride arose questions. That wasn't an ordinary stop. They were looking for something. I knew right then and there, everything had to shut down. Temporarily at least.

I was silent the rest of the ride to Jack town. After dropping Ron off at his moms, I made my way to Donte's house. He wouldn't be too happy about the news. "I told you them bitches were hot. I knew they were onto me too. I thought by taking the backroads and shit, I'd shake em, but now we gon have to lay low. I'll be back up in a month. That should give them enough time to get off my ass." I said to Donte. "Damn bruh. That's bad for business." "I know, but shit, I wasn't expecting this. They caught me off guard yo,"

"Yeah, I already know. I thought you were bringing Ron with you," Donte said. "I did. He wanted to see his mom and shit, so I told him I'd pick him up on the way back down." I looked up in surprise to see a Latina with the curves of a goddess walk in from the back room. "Helena?" I just knew my eyes were playing tricks on me. I knew my nigga wouldn't set me up with the bitch he was fucking with. "Isabella, her sister," she laughed sitting on Donte's lap. "I told you they were twins dawg," Donte said. I shook my head. "Where she at anyway? She must've gotten back with ol boy. She don't fuck wit a nigga no more." Isabella called her sister to see if she was busy. She said she couldn't get out tonight and I already knew what time it was. "I told her that fool ain't no good, but she loves his dirty drawers." I wasn't really checking for shorty anyway. She was just a distraction whenever I was in town. Isabella stood and said to Donte, "I'm heading out. Kiesha's on her way to pick me up. We're going to the mall and later the movies," After kissing Donte and collecting some spending money, she was out the door.

"Damn, so you moved Toya out and Isabella in huh? My nigga," We sparked up a blunt, as we started a new game of 2K. "Hell yeah, shit just kept getting worse. Toya followed me to Issa's dorm one night. To be honest, I didn't know how much I would miss her ass, until she was gone. Bitch won't take my calls. Then on top of all that shit, Issa ass pregnant." "Damn, now you know better than that bruh." I couldn't believe my round was fucking up like this. He knew the rules of the game. Hell, he taught me. "I know man, I know. I was wearing a jimmy mane. It's just messed up."

"I guess everybody fucking up home bruh. Belle found out about ole girl from school. I been at Nana's house for almost a month." I said shaking my head. "You better take advice from me. Cut that other shit off, focus on ya fam. She'll be here today, and gone tomorrow." I knew what he was saying was true, but for some reason, I just couldn't keep her off my mind. "Speaking of this chick. This her calling me now. Hold on bruh," I paused the game to answer my phone. "I thought yawl weren't together T. You said, you didn't even stay with her anymore. Why you always fucking lying." I just let her yap, since the truth was bound to come out. So, yeah, I did tell a lie or two dealing with her, but I didn't expect to still be fucking with her. She was catching feelings. I knew it, but It had gotten to the point of no return for me. Her shit was like a poison that I had been injected with. I tried to do more things to pour my feelings into Belle, but the more I pushed, she pulled away. "I'm done with you bruh. I'm so fucking serious. I don't mind helping you from time to time, but that other shit? That's dead." I couldn't argue with her. I got caught up. I knew eventually she would find out.

"Listen Sin, I'm out of town right now. When I get back, I'll make it up to you. I know I fucked up ok? Just give me a chance to straighten this shit out." When I realized I was talking to myself, I looked at my phone to see, she had hung up on me.

****

As soon as I made it within Gulfport's City Limits, my mind was filled with thoughts of Sinclaire. Ron and I had been drinking the whole ride. I happened to be a sober driver. I just had to see her. I knew it was late, and she'd probably be sleep, but I didn't care. I decided to try my luck and knock on her window.

When she came out in a t-shirt with no bra, my eyes immediately went to her chest. "Come ride wit me," I said. Our eyes were locked, and I could feel the passion emitting from her body. "Ok." Then I say, "And Wear that," I pointed to her shirt.

I was going to take her to my G-ma spot, but she insisted we do it in the car again. "I just feel so adventurous with you. I feel free to do whatever, whenever." She said.

We made love to the sounds of Usher's Bedtime playing on my speakers. She felt so good. I could hear her in my ear, "Go deeper baby," I did. Then she said, "Kiss me" As bad as I wanted to in that moment, I knew that would be the crack that broke the camel's back. I would no longer be able to run from her. I couldn't give in. Even though I knew I was playing with fire by keeping her and my family. I just didn't want to let go. I could feel her fingers digging deeper into my skin as I brought her to climax. She kissed me softly, as I fought the urge to satisfy the need within me.

<u>**Ch. 13**</u>

Sin

Give Thanks

"I don't know. You know your moms don't like me bruh." Tommy said. I don't know why my mom was always so hard on him, but that's exactly why she doesn't know I've been seeing him. I had invited Tommy to eat with us for Thanksgiving. I knew Belle hadn't allowed him back home yet. He would be all alone for such a family oriented event. I tried to convince him. He was a hard nut to crack. "I can just hear your aunt now. 'So this ya boyfriend huh?' Checking out my stats and shit. You remember how she did me the first day she met me. I don't know Sin, I'll think about it. Ma Dukes can throw down though," We laughed. He knew my mom could throw down in the kitchen. If anything, I knew he would come just for the food.

"Just think about it, ok? Oh yeah, and thanks for the ride. I know my mom really appreciates it. She says she's working on getting me my license, but she works so much, I don't know if we'll ever get around to it." He smiled and said, "It's cool. Don't sweat it." I don't know what came over me, but the urge to kiss him, was on my lips. It happened so fast. I quickly apologized. "Sorry." As I hurriedly reached for the door handle, he reached out to grab my chin, bringing me in for another. I was so wrapped up in his kiss, I didn't notice my sister knocking on my window. That was our knock back to reality. I rushed out of the car, snapping at my sister.

As I watched him drive off, I said to my sister, "What happened to privacy?" She laughed and said, "Yawl were kissing in front of the house. How much privacy did you expect?" Damn, she had a point. I looked at her outfit and said. "Where you goin?" She looked around as if our mom was in distance and said, "I'm about to go to this party. Ma, thinks I'm going to the movies with my friend. Can you cover for me?" I smirked and laughed. Her little sneaky ass. She knew I couldn't say no because she had been holding my secret all this time. I said, "I gotcha, but you gotta give me the exact address of the party, and call me periodically to make sure you're ok. If at any time it takes too long for me to hear back from you, you already know I'm coming through, guns blazing yo." We laughed. Her friends pulled up a few minutes later.

As I watched her leave, I made sure I got a good look at all her friends, before they pulled off. I was very protective of her. Only because I had such a hard time growing up. I never wanted my sister to go through any of the things I endured in life. The street life was no place for a sheltered girl like Latavia.

I went into the house to find my mom cooking lasagna. I smiled bright and said, "Umm, something smells good Ma," she swatted my hands as I tried to sneak a taste. "Now you know better than to be in my kitchen bothering me while I'm trying to cook. What's wrong with you anyway. You're all happy and jittery," I laughed and said, "Ma, you always think cause I'm happy, something gotta be going on. I'm good. I just had a good day today. Is that alright?" I said with a smirk. She went back to fixing her food. Paying me no mind. As I sat and watched her cooking, eventually she made me help. "No sense in you sitting here watching me slave. Wash your hands and grab a pan from the bottom of that cabinet." I looked up smiling as I buttered a second casserole dish for the potato au gratin. Mom liked to cook everything from scratch. She was an old-fashioned cook. She learned all her tricks and training from my granny. I said, "Ma, I invited Tommy over for Thanksgiving. He can't be with his family and we've got plenty of food. I just wanted to be nice." She looked at me skeptically. "Why won't he be with his own family?" I froze. I didn't want to say too much, but then again, I had to sell her on the idea, because I had already invited him. "He lives with his grandma, and she won't be cooking. She'll be out of town. Her daughter invited her to Memphis." The words just rolled out. One after another. I'll have to fill Tommy in on them when I see him, so that they won't catch us in a lie. I laughed to myself. I wasn't sure if she bought it, but she went back to stirring the pot on the stove. I said, "So…. Is it ok Ma?" she said, "Uh huh. Just tell him, I'll have my eye on him. You know I don't trust his black ass." I smiled and said, "Yes ma'am."

Later that night when Latavia had returned from the party, I was anxious to find out how it went. I said, "Ok, spill. What happened B," She laughed and said, "I knew your ass would still be up. Thanks for looking out though. You already know it was booming. Every party Percy puts on, it always goes down." She started telling me how the night went. There were guys everywhere. I was glad she didn't go by herself. She was one of the youngest in attendance. She said it started out pretty slow. No one wanted to dance. All the men were lined up on the walls, while the girls stood around in clicks chatting about random shit. She was ready to go by ten thirty. By the time eleven o clock hit, the spiked punch had started to liven up the party. She was having so much fun dancing with her friends. They partied for hours until the drama broke out. This girl caught her man getting it in, in the bathroom with some jump-off. As soon as they started fighting, it lead to everyone throwing blows. Everyone was knocking each other over trying to get to their cars. "It was a mess girl. Ya boy was there too. I caught him rushing out behind my crew," she said laughing. That didn't surprise me one bit. I knew that was his type of scene. "I'm just glad you had a good time, and came back in one piece. Go wash up, and change before you wake mom," I said while pushing her out of my room. She rolled her eyes and closed the door behind her.

******

The aroma in my grandmother's house was filled with spices and exotic odors. There were so many different dishes being prepared in the kitchen. I couldn't stop my stomach from grumbling. I was starting to worry that Tommy wasn't going to show. It was almost time to do our traditional prayer and give our thanks around the table before we ate. I didn't want him to miss it. I was in the kitchen with the ladies putting the finishing touches on the food. "Grab the potato salad out of the refrigerator Sin. I'm not trying to hear nobody fussing about no damn taeta salad." Grandma called out to me. It was so crowded in the kitchen, I could hardly see the fridge, much less get to it. After retrieving the salad and placing it on the table, I noticed everyone grabbing hands to start the prayer. Just as my uncle was starting to pray, I heard the downstairs door open. It was Tommy and Ronte. I smacked my lips and said, "Why would you bring him?" Tommy rushed up to me and said, "Calm down bruh. Why you dissin my man?" I frowned at Tommy. He knew I didn't like Ron's Pretty Ricky looking ass. "You know Kelly's here too. All they gon do is fight, and my grandma does not play that shit." Folding my arms, I looked Ron up and down. "I ain't on no bullshit today Sin, I come in peace," he said raising his hands laughing. I rolled my eyes and walked off to go join the circle. As we were praying around the table, Tommy was twiddling with my thumb. I tried not to laugh, but he always chooses the wrong times to act out. I could feel my granny's eyes on me from across the room. I squeezed Tommy's hand and motioned toward my grandma. He got the picture, and closed his eyes again.

Once everyone had eaten and bellies were full, my mom said I had to do the dishes. I hated getting stuck with the dishes for holidays. It was always stacks upon stacks of pots and pans. As soon as I started, my cousin Rhonda came to help me. That was a surprise. The surprise didn't last long when I found out why she volunteered. She was wondering who my friend Tommy was. I shrugged and said, "He's a friend of the family. Why? Your hot ass is pregnant. You don't need any other distractions." I laughed. She was drying dishes, while I washed. "Hell, I'm not far enough along for anyone to tell. I'd ride him into the sunset bitch," I splashed a handful of suds on her and laughed. She's so nasty. "You don't want him anyway, Sis. He's married." I waited for her to close her mouth from shock, and said, "Hell yeah, he cute though, I can't even lie," I was lying my ass off. I knew Rhonda would hop on Tommy so fast, if he was down for it. I didn't need him messing with my cousin on my mental too. Even though I'm sure he wouldn't do me like that, but nowadays, I didn't know what to believe.

When I finished the kitchen, I went in search of Tommy. I hoped he wasn't causing trouble with my older cousins. When I noticed him on the porch talking with my grandmother, I paused to eavesdrop on the conversation. "My Sinclaire, is a special young lady son. I can sense loyalty and respect in your mannerisms, but your street mentality, I can't ignore. These are qualities I know can hurt my baby. I know yawl are more than friends. I can tell by the way you look at her. Where you choose to go with these feelings, is what concerns me. Something is keeping you from loving her. When a man can't present himself to a lady's family in a proper fashion, means he's hiding something. Which one is it: a child, a woman, or both?" Tommy shook his head and said, "A family. I love my girl Ms. Evans, but I'm in love with Sinclaire. I don't wanna lose my family, but I can't lose Sin either. I should never have let it get this far, but if I had it to do over again, I would." My granny was quiet for a spell. She rocked in her chair in deep thought.

When I thought she was finished, I turned and walked off in the opposite direction. As I walked off, I noticed everyone outside circling Kelly. Ron's back was facing me, but I could tell by the look on Kelly's face they were fighting. "How many times do I have to keep telling your dumb ass, I am not your man. Now you got your people all in ya business and shit." I rolled my eyes as I made my way through the crowd. Kelly said, "You were my man three weeks ago. What happened between now and then Ronte? Who's ya new bitch?" Raising his hands screaming to the sky, Ron said, "WE WERE NEVER TOGETHER! What is wrong with you girl? It was just a smash and dash. That's it. I'm not trying to fight with you bruh. I already told your cuz, I wasn't here on the bullshit. Just leave me the fuck alone please." As Kelly started to slap the taste out of Rons mouth, I grabbed her arm. "This is not the time, or the place. Did you forget where you are?" She was steaming. Red in the face, and ready to tear Ron to pieces. I could feel her embarrassment. She couldn't make him want her. That was clear.

Tommy had ran out front when he heard all the commotion. He grabbed Ron and said, "Let's roll bruh. I told you, don't start that shit at her people house." As they walked off, I heard Ron say, "I didn't start it. That bitch is delusional bruh. I think she a stalker, for real." Shaking my head, I turned back to snap at Kelly, but my Grandma had beat me to the punch. "Get your lil fast ass in this house girl," She said pulling Kelly by the ear.

<u>Ch. 14</u>

Ron

How Many Licks

"What the fuck happened Ronte?" Daniel said. I knew he would be mad. At least it wasn't my fault this time. "Blame your fucked-up ass timing. They pulled us at the wrong time. We were supposed to be on the way back when they stopped us." I was sitting in the local office wearing a hoodie and tan khakis. I didn't want anyone to see me when I snuck down here. I was on the phone with Daniel while Parker was burning a hole into the floor of the office. "It just doesn't make any sense? Why would they stop you all heading to Jackson, when I specifically told them to catch you all coming from. I gotta call Eddie and find out exactly what happened. Put Parker back on the line." By now Mr. Parker was mumbling to himself. I swear the nigga's crazy. "Yo, phone my dude." He snatched the phone from me and I could see the steam blowing through his ears. Whatever they were talking about was not good. I just sat back and laughed. At least no one can point the finger my way again. I was in the clear.

"I knew it was that new kid. Why would you send a rookie on a mission so important? Did he know how much was riding on this?" Parker was blue in the face.

Daniel had involved Parker in this mess and now it was both their necks on the line. Parker seemed to be a nerd. He wasn't trying to get caught in any of this off the record work. He worked hard for his stripes. I could read his thoughts as he continued pacing the room.

"Listen, I don't know about this Sir. I'm not even supposed to be working in the Narcotics division. Chief's been on my ass for the last two weeks. He's starting to get suspicious. I think we should close the case. We haven't been able to pin anything concrete on Mills," Parker stressed. "Now you listen to me you Prick. Must I remind you about these pics I have of your wife doing the Lambada on your neighbor James's cock? One word out of you and I'll have these online quicker than you can count sheep with those Bifocals you have on." Daniel screamed. Parker's nostrils flared as he said, "When this is over, I want every copy made. You told me you deleted those a year ago." I felt like I was sitting in on one of those old ass soap opera shows. Parker crying, and Daniel tripping. I propped my feet up on the table since, I figured I would be here for a while.

"We've got one more shot at this and damnit, I won't hear of any fuck ups." Daniel said to Parker. He was still steaming mad, but he listened in on Daniels new plan.

My cell began buzzing in my pocket. I went outside to take the call. I knew it was Tommy calling about work. If they knew I was talking to him, I'd be forced to record the conversation. "What's good Woe?" "Where you at round?" "Over on the southside. What's up?" T whistled and said, "Bruh, I just ran up on a lick. This nigga from the N.O, trying to put me on. He say that shit out there so pure my nigga. The coast ain't seen no shit like this dawg." I looked around nervously and said, "Oh yea? What it's looking like?" "Twelve a pop. You know I jumped on that opportunity bruh." I could hear his excitement through the phone. "I set up a meeting this weekend. I'll head out there to iron out the details and meet his connect and shit." I quickly said, "You want me to roll out there with you, fam?" "Nah, I'm good. I think its best if I go by myself. His connect might be funny and shit. I don't need no problems, ya feel me?" I nodded sweeping the parking lot in paranoia. Once we finished up the conversation and I was ending the call, I felt someone behind and cursed under my breath.

******

"Yo Ron, What up baby?" I looked over and saw Marcus heading my way. I was on break from class and heading to my car. He slowed to a jog and said, "Where you going for lunch?" I had planned on taking Alex for a quick lunch break. We didn't need any company. I shot him down quick. "I'm just catching a smoke break. Hell, I thought I'd never make it out of that mufucka." I said. He leaned on my car and caused me to snap. "The fuck are you doing? I just got a fresh wax on this bitch. You don't see me leaning on it, do you?" I said pushing him and rubbing the spot he had just occupied. "You need to chill the fuck out bruh. Don't nobody give a fuck about your little funky ass whip." I was two seconds from smacking this nigga. I thought twice about it. Although I knew he was the wackest nigga out the crew, he was definitely the strongest. I noticed Alex coming out of the school. When she saw me talking to Marcus

she went back inside. I shook my head. I had to get rid
of this dude.

"So, what's up man? What you need? I told you I was on
my way out." He gave me a nasty look, shook his head
and walked away. When I noticed the coast was clear, I
text Alex to come back to the car. She was wearing a
bright pink blouse with matching heels and jeans so
tight, it left nothing to the imagination. "You look good
boo," I said once she got in. She smiled and said, "Thank
you babe. Even though I'm at work, I try and keep it
sexy. David would never have let me out of the house in
this. He smothers me." I laugh and say, "It's cool. You
got me now. I appreciate every curve shawty."

We ended up at this expensive ass restaurant called The
Almanett. I started to tell her, this was too damn high,
but I knew she was probably used to this treatment. The
food was delicious though. It had better been, as much
money as I spent on the tab. I could feel her playing
footsie with my pants under the table. I was so happy I
finally got shorty to open up to me. She was freakier
than I expected. The things she did in the bedroom
made me question why she was married to a lame like
this David cat. From what she's told me, he's like a
robot in bed. He never pays any attention to her wants
or needs. She said she had never had oral sex from a
man before me. Looking at her, you would never expect
it. They've been married for ten years and he was the
first and only man she had ever been with.

Sometimes I wondered what made her change her mind about dealing with me. She was so shy before. I smiled at her across the table and said, "So you wanna play in these people's fine establishment huh?" She laughed. Her cheeks turned a rosy pink. "Why, I have no idea what you're talking about Mr. Ron." I licked my lips and said, "You'll know when we get back to your office Mrs. Alexandria. There's some things we need to discuss." She crossed her hands on the table and shyly said, "And what things might those be Mr. Ronte Smith?"

"I need you to help me remember, how many licks it takes to get to the center of the..."   before I could finish my sentence, Alex was up and out of her seat. "Well, it's time to go." I laughed getting up to join her. "Why you gotta act like that? Was it something I said?" She had already made it out the door.

We laughed, and play fought the entire ride back to the school. I was having fun making her squirm in her seat. There wasn't much she could hide from me at this point. I had her right where I wanted her. I dropped her off at the back of the school and came and parked in the front. On my way in, I ran into Kelly and Sin. I rolled my eyes. I wasn't dealing with the drama with Kelly today.

"Hey... um, can we talk?" Kelly said. I knew what direction this was heading in and I wanted no parts of it. "I'm kind of in the middle of something right now Kellz. I'll hit you up later." I started to walk off and she stopped me saying, "Ron, you can't just ignore me. I'll just keep asking until I get what I want. Will you give me a minute?" I didn't need her crazy ass causing another scene, so I told her we can talk in my ride.

"Make it quick," Kelly pouted as she got in the car and said, "I miss you boo. It's been almost a month since we've kicked it. I know you miss this good shit," She said seductively dancing in her seat. I paid little attention. "If that's all you wanted to talk about, then you're wasting my time. I told you, we're done." She rolled her eyes, flipped her hair and said, "Look, if you're not getting it from me, then who are you getting it from? You barely know anyone down here?" She really had the nerve to press me like she's my lady. I found this shit hilarious. "Yo, why are you pressing me? We're not together." I said laughing. "I know its some bitch named Alex, and once I find out who she is, it's a wrap." I wasn't laughing anymore. "What makes you think her name is Alex? If I was talking to someone, I don't tell anyone my business, so how would you know?" She smiled and said, "Don't worry about all that, just know that when I catch the hoe, she's mine." She said flipping her hair and stepping out of the car.

<u>Ch. 15</u>

Sin

Riding Down the Highway

"Come on Sin. It's my birthday weekend. I can't spend it with my kids, so you already know I wanna spend it with you." Tommy had come over to handle business with my aunt. We were play fighting on my couch in the living room, while my mom and aunt were talking in her room. "I don't know Tommy. I have my final exam in Craps on Monday. I really need to spend this weekend studying. You of all people should understand that. My skills are not as advanced as yours, and if I plan on passing, I have to keep my mind on craps." I said hitting him with a pillow. He laughed and said, "I got you. We'll have plenty of live action practice at the casino. I'll make sure we stop there on the way back. Just chill and let me take you away," He started singing, "Hey, let's get away. Let's get a room on the other side of town," I was too done with his goofy ass. Ugh, how could I say no to him. I roll my eyes and say, "I swear to god, if I fail this test, bruh." He was smiling from ear to ear.

Now I had to think of an excuse to give my mom. I had to make a few phone calls to cook something up. My cousin Christina was throwing a party this weekend and said I could use that as my decoy. I knew she would come through for me. As many good grades as I 've gotten her over the years, she owed me this favor. Once my mom had dropped me off at Christina's house, I went over the plan with her.

"Bruh, make sure anytime she calls, you answer. I am not trying to hear her tripping." Christina laughed. She was dressed in a pretty pearl sequin dress. I could tell she was ready to get crunk. She was turning nineteen. Her mom and dad were going all out for her birthday. I was a little jealous. I can't lie. "Will you chill out. If you run this plan by me one more time, I'll scream," she said. I didn't want to leave any details out, that's probably why I ran it back so many times. When I got a text from Tommy saying he was outside, I hugged the birthday girl and made my exit.

****

Riding down the highway, Four. Five on side me, Bad chick on side me, She roller coaster ride me - Boosie Bad Azz

As we rode down Interstate 10, heading to our destination, we were rapping along with our favorite rapper. There was something about Boosie that made you want to get reckless. His music just pumped your adrenaline. Every now and then I checked my phone to make sure my mom hadn't called. I couldn't believe I was really sneaking to New Orleans with Tommy. This shit is crazy. He saw my expression and laughed. He knew I was nervous as hell and shaking in my drawers. He rubbed my knee to calm my nerves. "Chill, your mom is not thinking about you right now. We made sure we secured our tracks. You're good." He may be at ease, but he didn't know my mom. When she got mad, she really got mad. I put my focus on the road to help ease my mind. As we neared the Louisiana state line, I noticed Tommy switching lanes. He was mumbling under his breath, so I couldn't hear him over the music. I asked him, "What's wrong?" When I noticed him pulling off the road I thought maybe we had a flat or something.

He took a bag from under the seat and told me, "Hey, don't ask any questions, just put this shit in ya pants real quick." He had lost his mind, "Why do you even have this on you?" I said. He pleaded with me saying, "I'll explain later, but just hurry up yo," I was so pissed off, but I knew the only way out of this was to help him. I couldn't believe I was risking my freedom.

It hadn't dawned on me just how stupid this really was, but I forced the drugs in my pants anyway. I sat uncomfortably while the officer did a mandatory stop and search of our vehicle. This was a routine stop whenever the patrolmen were looking for someone on the run. Once he cleared our vehicle and we were back on the road, I went in on Tommy. "Don't you ever do that shit to me again. You just basically said, fuck my future, fuck my career, fuck my life. Ugh, I'm so pissed wit you right now!"

"What else was I supposed to do? We both would've went to jail for the shit if I would've left it out. Is that what you want?" Tommy said. I frowned while looking out of the window in deep thought. I was steaming on the inside. I just didn't understand how he could jeopardize both our freedom by bringing that across state lines. The decisions he made were reckless. When he noticed I had tuned him out, he turned the radio back up as we continued our drive.

Once we made it to New Orleans, the sight alone was enough to take my anger away. It was something about the city that made me feel connected. Connected to what? is the question. Maybe it was because a lot of my family is from here. I've always loved the culture and freedom it possessed. Sometimes I would get this funny feeling in the pit of my belly, as if I was anxious for what was to come, because the town always held adventure.

When we made it to the hotel and was heading to our room, Tommy said, "I got a few runs I need to make. You go get dressed and we can go and hit the town when I get back." I frowned and said, "Yeah whatever," I knew what kind of runs he was going to make. He should've left all that in Gulfport. I knew this wasn't just a birthday trip he randomly wanted to take me on. I decided not to ruin the trip, so I bit my tongue on the matter. When we get back home, he was going to hear my mouth for sure.

****

We had hit a few night clubs on Bourbon Street, but most of them were busted for the night. My feet were killing me. I knew it was a bad idea to wear heels when visiting a big city like the N.O. I wouldn't make that mistake again. I told Tommy, "My feet are killing me. We need to find a spot, because all this walking is not the business." He spotted a small club and carried me inside.

He looked at me once we sat down at a table with a booth behind. I said, "You want me to pick her?" he nodded yes. I looked at all the bitches up on the poles and the ones walking around the club. I was looking for the one who caught my eye. Once I spotted her, I waved her over. She moved flawlessly in her six-inch stiletto heels. She had a long tattoo of a flower vine tatted down her side. Her body was curvaceous and creamy chocolate. She didn't have a blemish in sight. As she stopped at our table, I looked at Tommy for his approval and it was written all over his face.

I giggled to myself. When she came over to me, she bent down, and I whispered in her ear, "It's bae's birthday and I wanted to get him a lil show. Kiss me real quick," she laughed too. As she kissed me her flow of ebony locks cascaded down my face. I was only going to tease T, a little. Things had gotten kind of heated when she pressed her body into mine. She sat down on my lap, our lips still connected. I was getting hot. She started to move, and my lips took on a dance of their own. I slowly kept up with her and the beat.

She's a stripper, naked dancer, but she begging me to wife her…… From the first time I met lil mama, she was a one nighter…. Hell nah, Ion love em, but my money and my rifle. At the top like Eiffel tower, I told her to beat it, you'd a thought she was Michael. -Migos

As we continued to kiss, I felt her lift up and bounce back down, grinding on my lap. Then she quickly turned around and went to work on my lap. Giving me a full body lap dance. I bit my bottom lip and looked over at

Tommy, and he knew that look well. I was more than ready to get back to the room. I grabbed my glass of Apple Cîroc, T had ordered for me. Taking deep gulps as she continued to grind on my lap. T came over and sat closer to me. I guess he was getting a rise out of this. I stared at him reading his expression. Once I bit my bottom lip again, he grabbed it, kissing me with such force my body turned into an inferno. He took control of my mouth and our tongues were dancing in sync.

I had forgotten the girl was dancing on my lap, because the next thing I knew, Tommy had lifted me and placed me in his lap. Never once breaking our kiss. As I moved on his lap, in tune with the music, I noticed the switch in songs. "Bae,…. Mmmm, I'm ready to go when you are." I whispered in his ear. He said, while still kissing me and rubbing me all over, "Oh yea?" Once I moved to get up, I plopped back down in his lap and said, "Ooo, Bae, This my song. Just this one song. Let me dance for you, k?" While I started to dance in his lap, I sang the lyrics softly in his ear,

I'm seeing me on top of you….. Doing things that lovers do….. But I don't belong to you…. What's a girl supposed to do… Only need one night with you, to make all my dreams come true, You could never be my man … You can be my one-night stand.   -Oobie

I was working overtime on bae's lap. He was so into the song, I felt him get rock hard. I knew he'd always loved my singing. We were in our own little world inside of the dimly lit club. Our section was secluded. As I continued to grind for him, his hands moved to my center. I was panting and looking in his eyes by the next verse of the song, which I sang for him too.

Well it's about a quarter to three and no one's looking, it's just you and me,…….. You know I'm down for whatever and I aim to please, but its only for this one night……… Boy I hope that you'll come well with it, cuz I want you to know that I ain't never scared, You just make the rsvp and I'll be there, but its only for this one night….. One Night……..

As I made it to the chorus, I couldn't finish the song. Somewhere in the middle of that verse, Tommy's sneaky ass, had managed to slide it in. At first I panicked, because we were in a club full of people. When I tried to complain, he pushed farther, and my breath caught. There was no stopping now. My head rolled back as I rode him secretly in the dimly lit booth. I loved this adventurous side of Tommy. I knew I had fallen for him, and there was no turning back at this point. "Ooo, Tommy, Yes baby, yes, like that, Oh my g…." I screamed in his ear. That was a wrap for me.

Tommy was far from done though. He was anxious to get back to the room. I could see it in his eyes, he was going to tear this shit up. I laughed to myself.

<u>Ch. 16</u>

Streetz

Retribution

Once I made it back to Gulfport, and had dropped Sin off, I met up with Ron to handle a few loose ends. I had picked up new product in New Orleans. I instructed the squad on where they would distribute and how they were to lay low. "Marcus, you know you got a hothead my nigga, I really need you to lay low," I could tell Marcus was embarrassed when I singled him out, but it was true. Marcus was the hot tempered one in the crew. He's gotten us jammed up more than once in the few months he's been kicking it with me. I couldn't leave a risk like that up to chance, especially dealing with this new guy. He was all about his money. There wasn't any IOU's with this nigga. If you didn't come up with his money, it was lights out. I wasn't taking any chances.

When we wrapped up the meeting, I took JT with me to get started on the westside. Marcus and Ron were scoping out on the East. They took a few new cats with them. If I was to hit this deadline, I needed all the man power I could get. "Where you meet that nigga Ron G?" JT asked. I was pulling up at a local gas station. "You know my man Donte in Jackson, right? He put me on him while I was up there. Why you ask?" JT shook his head and said, "Something's off about that dude. He just gives me a bad vibe, you feel me?" I laughed and said, "You always paranoid about some shit bruh. You said the same thing about Marcus when you met him too. He's been solid since day one." Although I laughed, I was seriously considering what he said. I noticed some strange things about the kid too, but until I had something concrete, I'd let the fool breathe.

"Just relax my nig. Let me scope him out for a little and see where his heads at. I've been told sometimes I'm a little harsh on mufuckas. Just be ready if I ever give you the heads up though. It's lights out, friend or foe." JT nodded as he pumped the gas. On my way into the store, I noticed Kelly walking in behind me. I ignored her and stood in line to get a few packs of rellos. She came up behind me. "Hey boo. You getting me something too?" I smirked and said, "Nah, you good," she smacked her lips. "Why you always trying to play me? You weren't acting like that when I topped you off all those times. Keep on, and I'll tell my cousin what's really up. I know you like her, everyone can see that."

"Won't you mind ya fuckin business bruh. That's why I don't fuck wit you no more. You run ya fucking mouth too much." She grabbed me from behind and said, "Come on T, just one more time. I promise I won't say nothing." I snapped. "What the fuck is your problem girl? Don't be grabbing on me in public." I was three seconds from smacking this bitch. I had to get the fuck out of there before I went to jail. Fuck the rellos, I'll pick some up on the other side of town.

"Ya lady made it out of rehab yet?" I asked JT. We were sitting in the back of the trap house on the west side counting stacks. I could hardly hear his answer over the money machine. "Yeah, she's been out for about a week. It's been hard. Everything is a potential trigger for her. I think she may need a break from me, ya know? She doesn't need to be around this lifestyle anymore." I quickly said, "Nah, that's where you're wrong my friend. She needs you now more than ever. This is the most vulnerable she's ever been in her life. You can't desert her now. She'll just run back to what she knows. Then the whole process of the rehab would have been for nothing." I knew he loved her, because what man would stick around a woman for this long, through all her ups and downs, if he didn't. "You've made it this far together, you might as well stick it out." He shook his head and said, "Yeah you're right. I've known her for fifteen years, and I would've never thought we would be at this point in life. It's like, when things start going good for me, something comes knocking her down, and vice versa. We can't ever just be happy together."

For the short time I've known JT, this is the most he's ever opened up to me. I was used to, all work and no play JT. He was definitely showing me different. I had doubted my man. He's probably the strongest out of my crew. "Well my man, you know what you have to do. Lay low with the business when you're at the crib. Don't stay out too late in these streets. She'll need as much of your attention as possible. That's about all the advice I can give you on that, I've never been in that situation. I wish yawl the best though. Let me know if you need anything. You know I gotcha." JT didn't like handouts, but I had to offer. If he declined, that's his decision. I waited a few more minutes to see if he would change his mind. When it was clear he wasn't, I went back to counting money.

Once we were done and had gathered our material, my phone rang. It was Marcus on the line. "How's it looking over there? We broke the bank this way bruh," Marcus started rambling in circles and shit wasn't making sense. I told him to calm down and tell me what's going on. After he took a few breaths, his speech became clearer. "We got robbed my nigga! They emptied out the safe and everything. I don't know who the fuck it was. All I could get from the car was some out of town plates. Bruh I'm freaking the fuck out. It's about to get hot, and the mufuckas stole my ride. Come get us bruh, we gon hide out at Christina's house. Ron got fucked up pretty bad." My mind went from zero to a hundred. Of all the times for some shit like this to pop off, it had to happen with Terrance's shit. How could Marcus let this go down. He was one of my strongest soldiers. That's why I always kept him on my right hand. This wasn't some local niggas. I have my city on lock. They know not to fuck with me and mine.

We made it to Christina's house and the whole street was blocked off. It must have been a shootout. I called Marcus and told them to meet us in the back of Christina's yard. When they got in, I noticed Ron's face was fucked up. "Damn bruh, what the fuck?" Ron looked at Marcus pleading with him. I was confused. I said, "What's up? What happened?" Marcus then told us what went down. He said the boys went straight for the cash. "Something about Ron wasn't sitting right with them. They said he looked dirty, like an undercover or some shit. I tried to plead his case, but them niggas weren't hearing that. They jumped him bad and took it easy on the rest of us."

As I drove I tried to wrap my mind around where the hit could've come from. I knew It wasn't Terrance, because we just formed a partnership, he was testing me with his product. I asked Marcus, "You said you saw the plates whoa, what state were they?" As soon as he said New York, it all made sense. Big D's people must have gotten word about what went down, and they were getting back at us. I knew eventually I would have to deal with them, I just wasn't expecting it so soon. Fuck

Seemed like every time things were looking up, here comes another storm. We got to the stash spot and started going over different ways for retaliation. We had all the details on everyone in D's camp. The only hard part was trying to figure out who I would send up there to handle business. Marcus has clearly shown he can't do it. Ron is out of commission. That only leaves me with JT. With everything going on with his girl, it will be hard to convince him to go. I had no doubt in my mind that he could get things done.

"I have a plan. I need you two to heal and get yourselves together. We'll discuss the plan next week. Focus on getting your heads together too. Marcus, I'm disappointed in you my man." He ran his hand down his face and shook his head. I knew he was upset with me, but I had to be tough on him to keep him as my lieutenant. Adjourning the meeting, I let JT know I wanted to holla at him for a few minutes before he left.

"So, I didn't want to run the plan down in front of everyone, because I only needed you to take care of this one for me." JT immediately began shaking his head. He already knew where my thoughts were heading, and he wanted no parts of it. "Streetz, you know I'm down for whatever, but I just told you about my situation my dude. I can't just leave Cassie in her condition." I was two steps ahead of him. "You know I wouldn't ask you something like this, unless I had all that figured out. I was going to let her stay with my baby moms, until you get back. As tight as they are, Belle would have no problem." He ran his hands down his face, contemplating my offer. I knew this would be something he'd have to think over, so I told him, "Take your time and talk it out with your girl. Just let me know before next week. I'm trying to hop on these niggas as soon as possible. Ya dig?" He dapped me up and said, "I got you, Woa,"

<u>**Ch. 17**</u>

Sin

Distant Lover

I was so excited to show off my new car at school. My mom had finally taken me to get my license over the weekend. Now, I was free to drive my car whenever I pleased. It was an Altima. My dream car. I couldn't believe my mom when she surprised me with it this morning. I was blasting my music as I pulled into the school parking lot.

"Hey Sinclaire! Can I get a ride after school?" Nadine asked me. "She got her nerve." I said to myself. As long as I've been going here, she has never said two words to me, now all of a sudden, she needs a ride. Girl bye is what I wanted to say, but I said, "I can't, I have to stay for practice after class today." She was clearly aggravated with my answer, but I could care less. She walked off mumbling under her breath. See, that's how people do you. When you're lame, nobody fucks wit you, when you're up on your shit, You're that bitch then.

I noticed I was ten minutes late to class. Mr. James was not gonna let me live it down either. He's always bitching about me bruh. I swear, I don't think any of the other students gets harassed this much. At first it didn't really bother me, but now it's getting annoying. Like, damn, get off my shit yo. I managed to make it through the class. Gritting my teeth, the entire time. Lately I've been so moody. I've even snapped at my mom and sister. Must be that time of the month coming up. Ugh, just great. For break I noticed Kelly and Shay sitting at the table, so I headed over to join them.

"You ok girl? You been snapping on everybody. You can't be mad at that man because you were late to class," They laughed. I rolled my eyes and said, "Yea whatever. He's always picking at me, and worried about what the fuck I have going on. Like damn, I know what time class started. Can you get the fuck off my clit, damn!" Shay and Kelly looked at each other and bussed out laughing again. I was over it at this point. "Any way, what yall hoes been up to?" I said. "Girl, I think Ron has been fucking with someone else. Shit, if he's not getting it from me, he's gotta be getting it from somewhere. Ugh, and I hate how he's always in our advisors' face and shit." I shook my head and said, "Bitch, I been told you, you should let that clown go. He's a fuck boy. After he clowned you for Thanksgiving, I wouldn't even give his ass the time of day. Kelly, you have to start valuing your self more. That nicca does not deserve you. I'm sorry, but someone has to be real with your ass." Kelly is the same age as me. There is no reason she can't tell when a man is using her. I roll with her decisions, because she's my cousin, but enough was enough. Shay sucked her teeth and said, "If it isn't the pot calling the kettle black. You been sucking and fucking on Streetz, and it's obvious he doesn't give a damn about you either. Get your own shit together before you come for someone else," I was ready to smack this bitch. "First of all, Streetz is a single man, so whatever I choose to do with him, is my business. Second of all, I'm about ready to clap that ass bitch. Coming for me and I didn't send for you!" We both stood up from the table. "Chill out bruh. You trying to get suspended and we're almost at graduation. Damn," Kelly said stepping between us. I was done with this fake ass bitch Shay. I swear, it's like she's always talking out the side of her neck towards me. I knew a hater when I saw one. I picked up my bags and headed out to my car, where I waited out the rest of break.

****

"You always do this shit. You wait until damn near two o' clock in the morning to want to chill. I heard you were back with your baby moms anyway. Why the fuck you calling me?" I was heated. There was nothing he could say at this point. The damage was already done. If only I could stop thinking about his touch, and how he made me feel. I wondered if I would ever get over him. Any new man I pursued, would I still think of him? I had forgotten he was on the phone, when he said, "I had to. You don't know what it's like out here in these streets, Sin. Grams on that bullshit, so I had no where else to go. Shit, it ain't like I can come live with you. Just chill, come ride with me, and we'll talk about it ok? While you're at it, grab a blanket too."

I stare at the phone wondering what he has up his sleeve. Although I was angry with him, I was far more in love. Maybe it was lust. Hell, I don't know. At this point, I don't even think I know what love is. Whatever it was,

122

was making me grab my blanket and sneak off with him into the night.

"Where are we going?" I said when I noticed we were pulling up to a deserted part of the beach. I wondered how he knew this was my favorite place. It was the perfect getaway from everyday problems. I could sit out here for hours just listening to the ocean waves. He ignored my question. As we pulled up, I noticed a fire in the middle of the beach. There was no one around or in the water. "What's this? Did you do that?" He still didn't say anything. At this point, I just shook my head and got out of the car.

He placed my blanket on the sand and sat Indian style in the middle. I guess he was waiting for me when he looked up at me. I laughed and sat down as he wrapped his arms around me. "I brought you out here to watch the sunset wit me, is that alright?" A lot must be on his mind. He was usually on his gangsta shit with me. There was that comfort thing again. Every moment we spent together was always so calm and comfortable. We never had to say anything to one another.

"What's on your mind?" I asked. He took a moment before he said, "I don't know Sin. Shit's been getting serious between us. I can't get you off my mind. You know I don't even talk like this and shit. You changing a nigga," I didn't say anything because I was feeling it too. He never spoke his true emotions to me before, but I could always feel them. The trip to N.O. was amazing. I had never met that woman before. He was definitely changing me. I didn't want him to know, so I said, "As long as you're still living with her, I don't think there's anything for us to talk about," I had made up my mind. I was no longer going to have sex with him. I had to value myself more. On the drive over, all I could think about was how I was going to break it to him before he sucked me in with temptation. He pulled me closer because he knew I was right. He knew how he was treating me was wrong, and I didn't deserve it. I could read him like a book. I mean, he had become my best friend. Of course, I never wanted to let him go.

I kissed him with everything in me, because I knew it would be our last kiss. He looked me in my eyes and said, "I love you Sin, and you're right. You don't deserve to be treated like this. Just give me a minute to get my shit together." I leaned back into his embrace once again. We let the ocean do the rest of our talking for us, as we watched the sunrise.

****

I had to pick my mom up from the beauty salon. She always kept the same appointment every weekend. I was frustrated because I was only running off four hours of sleep. Even though Tommy and I let the time pass us, I was happy we had a chance to talk things out. Now that there's an understanding on things, hopefully this cycle would stop.

"Hey pretty lady," I looked up to see a tall guy looming over me. I was waiting in the front lobby of the salon. He was handsome, had a football player's build. He wasn't really my type. I decided to humor him anyway. "What's good?" I said, looking past him to make sure my mom wasn't walking up. I didn't need her all in my business. He smiled and said, "I'm just wondering what a brother like me has to do to get to know you," I smiled and slyly said, "Why would you want to get to know me? You seem like a fly guy. There's plenty of women here," I expected him to turn around and look at the other women I spoke of, but his eyes were glued to me.

"I'm actually on the job, so I wouldn't say I've been pursuing any women at the moment. The name's Cassidy. I'm a barber." I didn't know if I should be flattered or insulted, so I said, "So, what was it that you saw in me? What made you want to get to know me?" I laughed. Even though his punch lines were corny, he had my attention. I liked his courage. "You seem like you're more than meets the eye. If my thoughts are correct, you're trying to figure me out right?" he said smiling. Ok, yeah, this is a dead end. I decided to cut this convo short. "Well, my mom will be done in a moment, so I'd better get back there in case she needs my help. It was nice meeting you." I said grabbing my things before he tried to stop me. He grabbed my arm and said, "Can I call you sometime? Just to talk. You know, get to know you if that's ok," I rolled my eyes hard on the inside. I ran off my name and digits, just to get him off my back. I barely talk on the phone anyway. I figured there was no harm in that. When I noticed my mom walking towards me, I waved goodbye.

Ch. 18

Sin

In Love with Another Man

It's about to go down today at school. I already know what's gonna happen. With the news I have for Kelly, shit's about to hit the fan. So, according to Tommy, the bitch Kelly has been looking for is none other than our School Advisor, Mrs. Alexandria. Her name is Alex for short. I don't know how we missed it. I mean, I just never thought a married woman was who he was fucking with. I really didn't think Ron had it in him. I laughed to myself. "This is just too much," I say to Kelly when I run into her in the break room.

She looked at me crazy, "Why wassup?" I shook my head and said, "Now Kelly, I got some shit to tell you, but you gotta promise you won't trip. You know we're at school and they won't hesitate to kick our asses out. At least wait until after the graduation ceremony today. I got your back regardless though. You know if you bang, I bang." Kelly started laughing and said, "Bitch, spit it out. What the fuck are you talking about?" I couldn't beat around the bush anymore, so I just blurted it out. "Ron been fucking with the advisor. Her nickname is Alex. The shits been going down under our noses all this time. Obviously, her cousin is Roxanne. We owe both those bitches a beat down." Kelly looked at me to see if I was joking for a second. Then all hell broke loose.

She found Alex in her office and from there commenced to whoop ass. I was right there as promised. I was mad as fuck though, because I knew this would mean we would miss our graduation ceremony. Oh well, shit, they can't take away my degree. I earned that mufucka. I just won't be able to walk across the stage with my class. As Kelly and I were stomping Alex's stomach in, I felt someone pull me away. I looked up and it was Tommy. "Nah, get the fuck back. This dumb hoe deserves the shit. She all in her face flossing and shit wit Ron. She betta take these hands wit the same energy." I yelled trying to break away from T.

I saw someone grab Kelly as Tommy dragged me outside. "What the fuck are you doing? We're supposed to be walking today, and now you're probably suspended. Following behind yo cousin dumbass." I rolled my eyes and said, "So, that's my fuckin blood. If she bang, I bang. They gotta give me my degree. I just won't be able to walk the stage." Tommy shook his head and said, "You's one dumb mufucka yo." I watched as he walked off. When I noticed our Dean Mr. Robinson coming our way, I looked at Kelly who was still steaming on the inside, I knew what was to come. I stood up to greet him.

"Ms. Sinclaire and Kelly, I hate that it has come to this, because you both were doing so well. Disciplinary action must be taken. I must expel you both. Yes, you will still receive your degrees, but you won't be able to participate in our ceremony tonight. You also will no longer be able to come and practice whenever you get a dealing job. You both are banned from the campus."

Kelly and I walked off to my car. I told Kelly I would drop her off at home. When I made it to my car, I noticed Tommy standing in front of my door. He looked at me intensely. I rolled my eyes, because I hated when he did that. He was basically giving me the silent treatment and I had to figure out what the problem was. "Bruh, I'm not in the mood right now. What's up Streetz?" Whenever I called him his street name, he knew I was serious. He took his time, walked around me to sit on the hood of my car and said, "I heard about your lil boyfriend Cass," Rolling my eyes, I said, "The hell? I don't have a boyfriend."

"Cassidy, the barber, right?" You would've thought I had seen a ghost when I heard Cassidy's name roll off Tommy's tongue. How the hell does he know about Cass? "I went to get my shit lined up yesterday and ran into your boy. He told me all about his girlfriend that goes to the dealers academy. At first, I wasn't sure he was talking about you, but when I asked him your name, it made sense." I knew I had fucked up. My luck always tends to run out. What was the odds that T would run into him. Technically, I didn't do anything wrong. I've never even had a phone conversation with the nut. He blew me up all the time, but I was never home. I told my sis to tell him I was gone. Who would've thought this shit would get back to Tommy? Ugh, I'm so done.

"That nigga is not my boyfriend. He talked to me for like five minutes yesterday. Then blew me up all night. I don't even know that mufucka," Tommy had walked off in the middle of my rant. I knew he was pissed. I hadn't entertained another man the entire time we were messing around. I don't see how he could be mad though, he had a whole baby mama at home. He needed to get over his self. I rolled my eyes getting into my car. Kelly was on the phone cursing Ron out, as I pulled out of the parking lot.

****

Kelly wanted to chill at my house for a while before I brought her home. It was cool with me, because I had a call to make once I got there. I was so pissed off, I speed dialed that fools number. He had me all the way fucked up. I can't believe I let this nigga, fuck everything up. "Hey Sunshine," He sang in the phone. I rolled my eyes and said, "What the fuck is your problem? Why are you telling mufuckas I'm your girlfriend, when I don't even know your ass. We had one conversation." I guess I had taken him off guard, because he said, "Uh, I -I didn't know you felt that way. I thought we had a connection." This nigga. I'm really trying to be nice right now, but he is making it hard to do so.

"Dude, I don't even know you. You don't know me, so what the fuck are you talking about? I'm in love with someone. I didn't mean to lead you on." He was stuttering and stammering over his words. "Why don't you want to be my girlfriend? I love you hun," I couldn't take it anymore. I spazzed. "I never told you I wanted to be with you! You've ruined everything by opening your damn mouth! Now he barely talks to me and it's all because of you! I don't wanna talk to you anymore! Stop calling my fucking phone!" I slammed the phone down in his face and Kelly said, "Damn bitch, angry much?" I laughed but I really wasn't in the mood. I was so upset. "Yo, I had never seen that look on Tommy's face before. I wouldn't be surprised if he never spoke to me again. Fuck!" Kelly rolled her eyes and said, "Girl, that nigga love you. You know he ain't going anywhere." Sitting down on the bed beside Kelly, I shook my head and said, "Nah B, I really think it's over. Maybe it's for the best though. I've been feeling sick and shit lately. I can't be around him right now. If he thought for a second, I thought I was pregnant, he would flip," Kelly laughed and said, "Haven't yawl heard of condoms?" Side eyeing her, I said, "I know you ain't talking. What number you on now?" She pushed me off the bed, laughing. She knew I was right. Hell, she just had her fourth kid last year.

"Girl let me take you home, before my mom gets back. You know she'll be sweating me about curfew and shit." I usually had a twelve o' clock curfew, but lately since I've had my car, she's been letting me slide. It's usually because she's asleep before twelve, so she doesn't even know what time I come in. Once I dropped Kelly off, I stopped by my aunt Gracy's house. I was trying to see what was up with Brandon's sexy ass. My cousin Sherell introduced me to him a couple of weeks back. I really didn't give him any play because of my situation. Now that shit has gone left with Tommy, I'm back on the market. Nothing wrong with testing the waters.

"What's good girl?" Sherell asked before I got out of the car. I could read her expression. Bitch was trying to get out of the house. "Not shit. You heard from ole boy?

Tommy trippin, So I'm trying to see what's up with B wizzle," I said laughing. Sherell hopped in the passenger seat and said, "Girl hell yeah. You know my nigga over his house right now. Let's go shoot the shit," I damn near snapped my neck and said, "I hope yo nigga got some gas money. You do know he stay in Biloxi right?" She laughed and said, "Girl hell yeah, he got you. Don't even worry about it." There was no way I would see that gas money. I can't stand broke niggas. Brandon will be in for a rude awakening if he's broke too.

We pulled up to a house in the suburbs. I was confused, because Sherell was always fucking with broke niggas. I really had a hard time trusting Brandon wouldn't be the same. "This is Brandon's house?" Sherell rolled her eyes. "Yeah, his people got money and shit. He always flashing his doe. Like, nigga don't nobody care." She must be jealous or something. I shook my head as we got out of the car.

"What's up Babe, this is my cousin Sinclaire. You remember her, right?" Sherell asked her boyfriend Nick. He was a tall, brown, hunch back looking dude. Tattoos all over. He looked like bad news. I don't really comment on my girl's boyfriends, but this is just ridiculous. I couldn't see how he and Brandon were friends. Brandon was on the couch playing video games. He seemed like such a nerd, but a cute nerd though. I was laughing on the inside. "That's my cousin Brandon on the couch." I smirked and sat next to him.

He looked at me for a second before turning back to his game. "Well, we gone leave yawl up here to get to know each other." Sherell said turning towards the stairs in the back. I looked at her like, "Bitch, don't forget about my fucking money bruh," she read me loud and clear. Fuck around and get left in Biloxi if she want to.

"So, where you from lil mama?" Brandon said. "I stay in Gulfport. What about you?" He was so into his game, I had to repeat my question. He was already pissing me. I've been here five minutes and he's already ticking me off. "Oh, shit, I'm from New York. I came down here with my brother." I shook my head and said, "Oh ok. That's wassup. How long you been down here?" "A little over two years. You got a man boo?" I knew that was coming. "It's complicated. What about you?" I couldn't stop staring at his hair. He had long jet-black hair down his back. He must be Indian or mixed. Either or, he was fine.

"I got a lil shorty, but it ain't serious." He was lying. Ol girl probably in a fully committed relationship. "Yawl dudes are something else. You know that girl think yawl are serious. This is how yawl get shit started." I said laughing. He looked at me and bust out laughing too. He couldn't even keep a straight face off that lie.

We hung out for a good three hours before my mom started blowing me up. I was mad as hell. She would usually be sleep by now. Someone had snitched that I had my young cousin Sherell with me. She had school in the morning. "Yes ma'am. We're on our way now." I rolled my eyes as she rambled about expecting more from me because I was the oldest. I swear I'm always in trouble about something.

As Sherell and I headed back to the house, all I could think about was Brandon. How did someone like him get caught up with a rough neck like Nick. The shit just didn't sit right with me. I bet he has like five kids between here and New York. I laughed at the thought. "Girl, what you laughing at? You know your moms gonna kick your ass when you get home." Sherell said. "Yea because of your young ass. Why you didn't remind me you had school in the morning?" I already knew the answer to that. Her hot ass just wanted to spend time with Nick. Ain't no telling what they were upstairs doing. Sherell read my mind and said, "Mind ya bidness cuz, Mind ya bidness,"

Ch. 19

Streetz

Like A Thief in The Night

"Kelly been showing out lately. Ever since she fought Alex, she's been talking reckless. Talking about she gone get her brother to beat my ass. I ain't stuttin her brother. Who the fuck does she think I am?" Ron was bitching about Kelly again. As much as he says he can't stand her, his ass is always talking about her. I try to be sympathetic but the shit's getting annoying. "I don't know my nigga, I thought you stopped fuckin wit her?" He rolled his eyes and said, "I did, but hell, I can't get her off my jock. She calls me like fifty times a day. It got so bad, I had to change my number." We were posted in the hood on the corner. There wasn't too much traffic for a Saturday.

I had two shooters in hiding around me. Since that last stunt with D's people, I didn't want to take any chances. As I tuned Ron out, I tried to focus on my business at hand. I made an appointment with my supplier for next week. I decided to pay him the little money that was stolen back out of my own pocket. Once we have our last face to face, everything should be copasetic. I had to move my family out of this area. It's starting to get too hot. Everything had gotten out of hand. Things with Sinclaire will eventually explode if I don't nip it in the bud now. Belle's about to drop the baby, and I just don't need to give her even more things to worry about.

I realize I have to do what's best for my kids. At this point, they're all I got. It's time to put this childish shit to rest.

My phone starts ringing as Ron finishes his ranting. "What up?" It was JT. He was calling to let me know he had handled our situation in New York. It was a bitter sweet feeling. I mean, some one has to handle the dirty work. At the same time, wiping out a nigga's bloodline was never a part of the plan. Anyone can get it in the game of war. He let me know he should make it back by tomorrow sometime. I wasn't too worried. As long as I had my shooters around me, everything should run smooth. "You know Cass won't tell me, but how's she holding up since I been gone?" I took a deep breath and said, "She's good my man. I told you, everything's cool." What I didn't tell him was that she's been sneaking out every night. Where she went, I don't know. I never asked her, because she would always be back by morning.

I couldn't tell JT about it, because I needed him to handle business first. I'll just speak to him about it once he gets back. In the meantime, I gotta figure out where she's been sneaking off to at night. I don't know if it's because she's not comfortable in Belle's house, or she's just not comfortable with me being there also. Shit I don't have a lot of time to figure this shit out. "That's good bro. I guess I'll hit you up when I touch down then. Let me see what the big apple has to offer," he said laughing. "Ight bruh. You keep warm in all that snow, ya dig?" "Always,"

✱✱✱✱✱

"I'll be back babe. I gotta see where she keeps sneaking off too every night. I promised JT I'd look after her while he was gone." I told Belle before heading out. Cassie was on her way out again and it was well past midnight. I knew it was a bad idea for JT to leave her the car. As I trailed her and tried to keep hidden between cars, I noticed she was heading downtown. Why the hell would she be going downtown?

When I noticed her pull into a local bar, I could already see where this was headed. I hope she isn't stepping out on my boy. I damn sure don't want to be the one to catch her. I noticed she was sitting at the bar talking to an older white guy. She was pretty comfortable around him, so I knew she was familiar with him. They also didn't look like lovers. I was seated in the back while I watched them converse.

I was beginning to think she was ok and started to leave when I noticed him discreetly pass her something under the bar. Hell nah, I knew I shouldn't have volunteered to be Mr. Nice guy taking care of his chick. JT's gonna flip his shit when he finds out his girl's relapsed. I storm over and snatch her up from her stool.

"Tommie, Yo what the fuck are you doing?" She yelled. I didn't want to attract any unwanted attention so I walked her outside of the bar. "First of all, I know I didn't just see what I thought I just saw in there. Did I?" She got really clammy on me and said, "I don't know what you're talking about. I just came to meet up with a friend." "Oh yea? What's in your hand then?" She dropped it to the floor, waved her hand and said, "Nothing, are you happy now?" I picked the baggie up from the ground. It was a small bag of ecstasy pills. Cassie knew that I would know these were gateway drugs. One pop of these pills would send her right back to the big gorilla on her back. I couldn't even say anything. I just shook my head. "Please don't tell J, I wasn't gonna take it. I had been coming down here every night, and it was like it was calling my name. Tonight, I caved, I swear that's all man."

"Let's go. I'll trail you and we'll talk about it in the morning. JT should be back by then." I watched her get in her vehicle and I followed behind her. I didn't know if I should tell Belle about this. Knowing her, she'd kick the bitch out before sunrise. Nah, I'll talk to her about it later, if at all. Damn, breaking this to J is not going to be easy. Not only is he gonna kick her ass, but mine also, for not keeping her away from that shit. This has become a hell of a day.

Chapter 20

Sin

Girl fight

"Granny, you sure that's all you need?" I've been at my grandmothers' house all morning helping her with chores she needed done. She looked at me shaking her head and said for the third time, "I am fine girl. You've refurnished damn near my whole house. Now if you don't get your tail out of here, I'm gonna have to grab that broom." I laughed and sprinted out the door, before she made good on her threats. I loved spending time with my granny. She was so easy to please. Anytime I did work for her she would always throw extra cash my way. I had just made another forty dollars.

It was Saturday afternoon and I was looking for some dirt to get into. I called up my friend Trina to see what she had going. She answered sleepily, "Hello," "Girl, wake yo sleepy ass up. It's Saturday hoe," She laughed and said, "I know damn well you ain't talking. You're usually in bed until twelve every Saturday. What's up though?" "Shit, I was trying to see what you had popping, but you're lame. You still in the bed," I said laughing. I could hear her talking to someone in the background "Bae stop. Give me a second" "All I need is a second... or five, ten. Hell, an hour," she giggled in the phone. "Ew, get ya nasty ass off my phone bitch. I know you got your own place now but dang, he can't let you have a phone call?" "Girl I don't know why he's playing. He knows he'll be late for work if he doesn't get up and start getting ready,"

My girl was living the life at eighteen. I wish my parents were rich like hers. For her sixteenth birthday she got a Benz. Graduation, a key to her own apartment. She didn't want to live on campus for college. I swear I be so jealous of the kid. We've been friends since middle school. Here I am, nineteen still living on a fucking curfew. I pulled up to the corner store. "I'll hit you later girl. Let you handle ya business and whatnot."

I hadn't been in the store five minutes before Tommy had popped up on me. We hadn't spoken since the Cassidy situation. I just acted as if I hadn't seen him. "So, we're just gonna keep tip toeing around each other?" he said behind me. I rolled my eyes and said, "I mean, what else are we supposed to do? I thought you were done with me and I was all kinds of bitches and hoes T?" He laughed. I didn't see anything funny so I finished with my purchase and headed out of the store.

When he grabbed my arm, I snatched it away from him and said, "Listen, I don't have time for these games you playing, my nigga. Now you said what the fuck you said. That's it. We good. Move around my dude. I'm done with this shit," I could hear the words leaving my mouth, but as each word was said, I also felt the pain. The look on his face said he felt it too. That was his problem. He never wanted to face the reality of his actions. I was not just gonna be a used coat on the wall he could keep coming back too. At the end of the day, he made his choice, and now I'm making mine. I wish my heart could hear what my mind was saying. For some reason they never can seem to connect.

I held my composure as I walked the rest of the way to my car. I could feel his eyes on me the entire time. It wasn't until I drove off that I broke down. I just didn't know how to get him out of my system. At this point, I hated love. I didn't know why it had to be so complicated. Everyone boasts about how great love is, but no one ever teaches you about the pain that comes from it.

Struggling with my thoughts, I didn't notice my cousin Yayo's car parked outside my house. It wasn't until I saw Kelly and Shay sitting in my living room, that I noticed. "What ya'll doing here?" I said. "Yayo had some shit to take care of, so he dropped us off over here. I told him we could've waited in the car, but you know he be on one." Kelly said laughing. I wasn't too happy about Shay being there. That bitch just rubbed me the wrong way. I nodded at Shay. She nodded back. That's what our friendship had become. A nod and goodbye.

I guess since they were already here, it was no sense in getting upset over spoiled milk. I'll just have to curse Kelly out later. We talked about the latest gossip around town. Our cousin Miley and her husband were headed for divorce. Talk about a couple I never thought would've been divorcing. I was shocked. They were like the Will and Jada in the family. It just made sense for them to be together forever. It just helped me realize that time didn't last always. If someone "Claimed" they loved you, time is too precious to wait on them to make a decision. Yes, my mind was still drifting back to that idiot. Ugh. I had to get out of the house or that's all I would continue thinking about.

Shay asked me if I could take her to Port City, over on the other side of town. She gave me gas money so I wasn't tripping. I needed the break anyway.

***

As soon as we pulled up to her friends' house, I immediately regretted my decision to come here. She had me in the worst part of the city. The red zone. Meaning, gunshots every night. I forgot who I was talking about anyway. I should've known she would've been on some fuck shit. I kept my thoughts to myself though. I figured we'd be in and out, so it wouldn't be that bad.

Oh no, this bitch decided she wanted us to come in and chill and watch a few movies while her friend was waiting on her kids to get dropped off. I swear this mufucka must think I'm a taxi or something. I pulled Kelly back outside when Shay entered the apartment. I told her, "Bitch, who the fuck is this chick? Why is Shay trying to play me right now?" Kelly just shook her head and said, "Girl, I don't know. Some white chick she been cool wit." Rolling my eyes, I turned and started toward her apartment.

This "friend" was a straight up junkie. If the track marks on her arms weren't proof enough, the way she kept shaking every five seconds clearly gave it away. I shot Kelly a look that could kill. Somehow, I always end up in some shit fucking wit these two. It's been this way since we were kids. I used to think it was because I just wanted to spend time with my cousin, but once I noticed the patterns, I had to cut it off.

The girls house was a mess. I mean, I'm surprised she was raising kids in this pig sty. Yeah, I think I'll be cutting this little trip short. As soon as her kids get here, I'm ghost. She looked me up and down. Already pissing me off because she was clearly judging me. I mugged her back. She said to Shay, "Wassup wit ya girls attitude?" I laughed and said, "I don't have an attitude. Obviously, you do." I cocked my head to the said for added flavor. Shay rolled her eyes and said, "She cool girl. Sometimes she can be a little boughie."

Did this bitch forget she was riding with me? I laughed and told Kelly, "You know what? Bitch, let's go. I'll show a mufucka quick who boughie," she laughed. When I got up Shay said, "I'm playin girl. Calm down. For real, her kids will be here soon. Dang, why you trippin?" I was not in the mood to be playing these games. Not to mention, my mom would be calling me any minute to see where the hell I'm at. I turned and said, "I'll give them twenty minutes, but my mom will be calling me soon, so I can't stay long," Popping her gum, Shay went back to talking to her friend.

"Annie, when you gone clean up? Every time I come over, you never have it clean," Annie put a movie on, and said, "Don't worry about my house. As long as my name's on the lease honey, it should be none of your concern." Kelly laughed, and Shay smirked. Little white bitch had flava. I also noticed she had an accent to her voice. I asked her where she was from, she said, "Uptown baby, East bank all day," I could always recognize a fellow creole accent. My family is from New Orleans. "How long you been in Gulfport?" she scratched her head and said, "Bout two, three years. I came out here to live with my boyfriend. He abandoned me and his two kids a year after I got pregnant with the third. Dead beat ass mufucka." I wanted to ask her if he was the cause of her using, but I didn't want to put her business on front street.

After about an hour and a half, I had looked at my watch for the third time in the last twenty minutes. Where the fuck were these kids because I was about to leave Shay's ass. "Annie, maybe you should call your sitter and see how much longer they gone be. I got shit to do bruh," By this time, I was ready to get the fuck out of there. I was so tired of getting bit by mosquitos, you would have thought I had strawberries smeared on my skin. Ole girl looked at her phone sitting on the table and looked back at me. She said, "Chill, chill. She'll be here soon man,"

At this point, the light bulb finally clicked on in my head and I realized these junkies had played me. Shay and her crackhead ass friend. Shay obviously just wanted to come over and get a few blunts in rotation. I wasn't smoking that shit, knowing her, she probably laced them. I got up so quick. I said, "If you're not in this 2010 Malibu when I pull off, you will be left." With that I left out the door. I was putting on my seat belt when they both hopped in. Shay was mad as hell. I didn't give two fucks. I was so pissed with her. Halfway into the ride, Shay says, "We gotta go back man. I left my purse on the counter." I was so sorry for her. "I told you, my mom called me. I can't turn back now." She went from zero to fifty. "Come on bruh, I'll give you more gas money damn. All my stuff's in my purse," she yelled. I slowed the car down. "I would hate to have to do it, but you can certainly walk back." Her nostrils flared, and she fell back into her seat. She was so mad you could see steam shooting from her ears. Serves her right, bitch had the nerve to play me. I drove them home, with her mad the whole way.

<u>Chapter 21</u>

Streetz

Friends To Foes

"A few things have changed. I'm gonna have to teach you the ropes now bruh. JT on that bullshit since everything happened with Cassie. For some reason, he blames me for her almost relapse. I don't have time for the shit. Back to business as usual. He'll come around after a while, I guess." Ron and I were driving around the neighborhood because I had a lot to show and teach him in only a few hours. "Sure thing, my nigga. You know I got your back." That's another thing I liked about Ron, he was always ready for whatever. He was a certified hustler. "Oh yeah, and we're meeting up with the connect tonight. So, we need to make sure you know everything there is to know before this. Are you sure you can handle it?" Ron laughed and said, "I told you, your good bro. I mean, you know I'm down for whatever, but I must ask, Why me over Marcus? Yawl been friends for years." I took a deep breath and said, "Marcus has always been my boy, and no doubt he's always been down for whateva. This position, he's not ready for. Marcus is meant for muscle and that's it. He knows his position and he plays it well. Ya feel me? Now if you feel it's too much for you, now's the time to let a nigga know. You know I don't play when it comes to

145

handling business." Ron shook my hand and said, "I got
you boss,"

When we pulled up to the first stash house, I said, "This
was my very first investment when I moved down here.
I knew I wanted to build. Most niggas get in this shit just
to make a quick dime. Shit, I got a family to feed. I gotta
get it in any way possible, ya dig? When I found out I
had a son on the way, I bought my second spot. The
money started flowing at that point. I had to do what I
had to do," Ron was staring out the window. "Are you
listening nigga? I'm not fucking talking for my health." I
flipped and slapped Ron in the head. "I'm sorry man, I
got a lot of shit going on. I'm good though, I'm focused."
"You better be. I'm taking a hell of a risk putting you in
this bruh. One fuck up and we all screwed." Something
about his energy was off. I could feel it. "I'm good my
man. No worries. I gotcha." As I schooled him on the
operation and how everything was run, his demeanor
reassured me he was the man for the job. The next two
spots were done in only an hour.

***

*Lights, camera, action, pose…. I know I'm looking good
for these hoes I'm like, …. People compare me to Pac so
off top I'm like…. This gangsta shit don't stop, when I
drop I'm like….*

-Lil Boosie

Club Thirty IV looked like something out of a movie. The
establishment was set in an old school theme. There

146

were bottle girls walking around to every booth. Excellent customer service. I was seated in a VIP booth with three ladies dancing for me. Ron was seated in the next, with two ladies of his own. The night was young. I was so lit. You would've thought it was my birthday. I knew I was gonna leave some good tips tonight. Marcus was still salty about me picking Ron over him, so I made sure I hooked him up. He had three girls in his booth, and bottle after bottle flowing. Occasionally I would check the time. Cane would be here in any minute. It didn't matter how much fun I was having; my mind was always on business.

"You need anything else boo?" The waitress asked me. "Yeah, bring me another peach Cîroc and a bottle of Ace of Spade." "Coming right up," she said with a smile. Shorty was sexy. Redbone with blonde extensions down her back, in a tight red dress with a blue apron around it. They sure knew how to pick their girls. She was supposed to resemble a black pin up girl. Since the theme of the club was set in the late sixty's. She made a damn good impression.

"Where the fuck is this nigga?" I said aloud to myself. Almost two hours had passed. Here I am, checking my watch for the umpteenth time tonight. Right when I was about to pull my cellphone out to call Cane, one of the front window workers made his way over to me in a rush. "Yo, Streetz, got a message for ya." He passed me a note that said for me to meet someone out front. I knew it was from Cane, so I sent him on his way. After letting the guys know I was stepping outside for a minute, I went out front.

"What's good?" I said when I stepped to Cane standing in the doorway. "I heard you hot right now bruh. Heard you on the radar. You know me folk, I don't fuck wit pigs. Get ya shit together and then holla back at me." He said. I didn't know what was going on, but the nigga refused to hear me out. I was talking to deaf ears as he walked out of the club. Something was going down and I didn't know where it was coming from, and from who. How did he even know what was going on in my camp is the question?

I stormed back into the club to collect my boys. "Whoa, what's the problem T?" Marcus yelled over the music. I was too pissed to explain. I gave him a look that said not right now. He caught on quick and pushed the girls off his lap. Ron was watching the commotion, so he jumped up too. Once we were in the car, they started with the questioning. "What's going on Tommy?" Marcus said. "What happened with Cane?" Ron said.

I was steaming on the inside. The fact that rumors was spreading about my camp like a wildfire didn't sit well with me. I was missing out on business and I needed answers. As I drove my mind was wandering. It seemed like things just kept falling apart. I had worked so hard to secure the connect and then it was pulled from under me without a warning. Cane was in New Orleans. If he got wind of whatever's going on, that can only mean one thing: Shit had hit the fan.

****

Walking in the house, I felt a cold chill. Something didn't feel right. The lights were off, and I could feel Belle's eyes on me from across the room. I flicked on the living room lights and there she was, in tears watching my every move. I took a deep breath and counted to ten. I wondered what she could be upset about now. When I walked up to her, she didn't say a word. She handed me her phone and sat quietly. I read through a few status's and looked confused. When she pointed out the one that caught her attention, I froze.

"I always knew you were lying, but this? Tommy, how could you?" I could feel my family slipping away. There was nothing to say. As I read the status over and over, I knew nothing I could say would fix this. The more I thought of losing everything I had built, the angrier I got. I was witnessing something I never thought I would see. Belle's tears were falling, and it was all because of me. I don't know how it got to this point. It's as if my heart is torn between the two. I never thought I would fall for her. We were just having fun. Never thought it would get this far. It just happened. We had this connection, I can't explain it. Fuck!

An hour later, I was fuming. I was about to light fire into Sinclaire's ass. Once I calmed Belle down, I went into the bathroom to curse Sinclaire out so Belle couldn't over hear the conversation. Five minutes into the call,

149

there was a knock on the door. I could hear Belle screaming at whoever it was. I wasn't worried about that right now, I was too busy trying to find out what this mess was all about. The next thing I knew there was a Boom and two officers had burst into the bathroom on me. I could hear Belle screaming and yelling, "What did he do? Where are you taking him?" as they carted me off to their car. I knew this was going to be a long night.

The most embarrassing part was that my baby girl had to witness all that. With all the commotion going on, she walked in on the scene. I had fucked up big time. They always say your karma comes back to bite you in the ass. This had taken the cake.

<u>Ch. 22</u>

Sin

Dangerously In Love

"Thank you for taking the time to help me refresh my skills, Mr. James." Ever since I was banned from school, I couldn't get in any practice to try to get a job. Now that I think about it, I regret the decision I made that day. I should've caught her ass in the hood. Anyway, I was at The Silver Slipper practicing in one of their back rooms. Mr. James had connects all along the coast. He told me if I could prove my skills to him, he could get me hired on the spot. I was so nervous. "How many rounds do I have to play each game?" he said, "One. I won't hold you all night. Just let it flow, ok?" I nodded yes, then focused on the game. The cards flowed through my fingers. It was the first time I truly felt like a professional card dealer.

Every drill Mr. James called out, I was on it. I was so focused on the game, I didn't even notice a man watching from the corner of the room. It wasn't until he walked over to the table tapping Mr. James on the shoulder that I noticed. "James, my man. How've you been?" I looked up and noticed he was wearing a work uniform. He must work here. I wonder if he can give me some pointers to get on here too. I was looking for a hook up in any way possible. James said, "Lenny, how long has it been man?" While they talked out their reunion, I went back to concentrating on the cards. When I heard James say, "Well here she is bro. Did you get a chance to check her out?" I popped my head up in surprise. He's here to see me? I was taken completely off guard. I'm glad I didn't get nervous and start dropping cards everywhere.

"Yea, I've been watching from the door for the last twenty minutes. She definitely has what it takes. Can you start tomorrow night?" Mr. Lenny asked shaking my hand from across the table. I jumped up and down with joy. "Oh my God, are you serious? I got the job?" He laughed and said, "Yes if you can let my hand go." I quickly dropped his hand in embarrassment. "My bad. Yes, I can be here tomorrow night. An hour before my shift actually." James was grinning from ear to ear. I could tell he was proud of me. "You are one sneaky son of a" He gave me that look and stopped me mid-sentence. I hurriedly grabbed my things and headed for the door. On the way out I said, "Oh, I forgot to ask. What time to be here?" Lenny said five p.m and I was out the door.

****

"That boy has been blowing you up since you left this morning. I don't know what's going on, but whatever it is, he wouldn't tell me. He just keeps asking for you." My mom said as soon as I walked in the door. I was still high off my good news. At this point nothing could bring me down. I was high off life. I finally got my dream job. Monday can't get here fast enough. "It's cool, I'll call him back later, but right now, Guess what?" I said

152

smiling from ear to ear. My mom laughed and said, "What girl, you know I hate the guessing game." I couldn't hold it in, I burst with pride and screamed, "I GOT THE JOB!" I was jumping up and down with excitement. I just couldn't contain myself. My mom was shocked when she said, "What happened? I thought you were only there to practice?" I said, "I thought so too, but Mr. James had set me up a secret audition. Mr. Lenny was so impressed with my skills, he hired me on the spot!" I grabbed my mom in a huge embrace. She knew how hard I had worked for this. As we cheered and laughed in celebration, my mom's phone kept going off. She passed it to me. I knew it was Tommy again. He had been blowing my phone up all day. My cell had ten missed calls from him. I had it off during my audition and had forgot to cut it back on in the car. Laughing and out of breath I answered, "Hello,"

"You pregnant?" My eyes bucked, and my body went cold. I had been taken completely off-guard. How did he find out? How does he know? I don't understand. I took a deep breath and replied, "What are you talking about?" He yelled and said, "I said, Are you pregnant?" I didn't want to answer. This was the worst thing that could have happened. My joy had been stolen with two little words. I walked out of my mom's room to finish talking in my room. It's not that I was trying to hide it from him. I was going to tell him in my own time. I quickly tried to avoid the subject. Calmly I said, "You need to calm down. I don't know what you're talking about." The calmer I tried to be, the more upset he seemed to get. "Bitch, If you don't answer the fuckin question, I swear to God, I'm pullin up! You don't fuckin know me! You don't know who the fuck you playin wit!" Overwhelmed and angry I screamed, "I don't know!" "What the fuck you mean, you don't know?" he said. Crying, I whispered, "I said, I don't know. I haven't been tested yet. I was going to tell you once I knew for sure."

He was so irate. Yelling all sorts of threats towards my family and me. This wasn't the man I loved. This wasn't the man I grew to know and trust. He had become a savage in this turn of events. All I could do was cry. I didn't know how I had gotten myself into this mess. I asked him how he knew. He said, "Watch who you run ya mouth to. That bitch Shay put it on facebook and now Belle knows." I hurriedly checked Shay's facebook page and there it was. She had blasted all my personal information for the world to see. I didn't know what to say to him. My mind had frozen in time. I returned the phone to my mom, grabbed my keys and took off. I took off to go whoop that bitch's ass and I didn't give a fuck who was at her house. I was just gonna walk in that bitch and drag that hoe out.

I can't believe I trusted this stupid mufucka. Looked at this bitch as my fam and she did some shiesty ass shit like that because of a fuckin purse. I had a feeling I knew who it was that told her, but I needed proof first.

I finally answer the phone for my mom and she managed to calm me down. I change directions and decide to ride down the beach instead. It was such a beautiful night. I loved to ride the beach at night. Soft and serene was how it looked. I start to reflect on everything Tommy and I have been through. I realize I can't go through a pregnancy with someone as dangerous as him. Could he really try and bring harm to me or my family? I started to question my trust in Tommy. Was he who I thought he was? Was all this just a front because he just wanted sex. I was confused.

One thing had finally become clear to me. I never thought of it before, because I never wanted to admit the truth. Even though Tommy was my everything, and I loved him with all my heart, I realized, I was his

mistress. I would always be number two. We were friends and lovers. Yes, he claimed me. Yes, he loved me. He was never ashamed of me. In his mind, I was never number one. As hard as the truth hurt, that was the pill I had to swallow.

My mind was all over the place. The more I thought of everything, the faster I drove. I could feel myself losing control. The more I thought of the hurt, the betrayal and the lies, the harder I pressed on the accelerator. At this point I didn't know where I would end up. I could feel myself blacking out as I did whenever my emotions got the best of me.

My mind was numb, and my heart was crashing. All I could hear were the cars honking as I passed them. How could I be so stupid? I knew he would never choose me. Why didn't I leave him when he first mentioned they were still together? How could you have let it get this far? Ughhhh, I fucking Hate Him!!!

I saw my phone lighting up from the passenger's seat. I didn't recognize the number, but I knew it was him calling me again. As far as I was concerned there was nothing left to say. I could barely see the road through my tears. I was even more angry at myself for crying over him. When it rang again, I decided to answer only to cuss his ass out. As I picked up the phone and said, "What the fuck do you want?" I could hear the car beside me honking again. I turned to flip him off as Tommy said, "Where you at? Some shit just went down. I'm downtown at the precinct. I'm in deep Sin," He was lying through his teeth. I knew he wanted to meet up to talk, which would only end with me giving in again. I had had enough of this back and forth. I just couldn't take it anymore. I was now at one hundred and five miles per hour. "I am so done with this Tommy. You're bipolar as fuck!!! You were just screaming about fucking me up a second ago, and now you want me to believe you got knocked? Fuck that and fuck you Tommy. I hate-

Skkkkkkeeee Booom!!!!!!

TO BE CONTINUED....